The Mountain of Gold

The Mountain of Gold

Ramesh Gupta

RESOURCE *Publications* • Eugene, Oregon

THE MOUNTAIN OF GOLD

Resource Publications
An Imprint of Wipf and Stock Publishers
199 W. 8th Ave., Suite 3
Eugene, OR 97401

www.wipfandstock.com

HARDCOVER ISBN: 978-1-7252-8068-7

For Amit,

a rare and noble man

For what shall it profit a man,
if he gain the whole world,
and lose his own soul?

The Gospel according to St Mark 8, 36 (KJV)

I

Many men do tell, of the Mountain Hell,
    where flows a river of gold.
But none return that I have learned,
    from aught that I've been told.
Both foolish and bold, for the sake of gold,
    they all have ventured there.
And so many have said, the souls of the dead,
    there leave their bodies bare.

The Mountain of Gold

When the moon is arisen, none dare listen,
    to the sound of demon song.
For in the forest, the wild wolves' chorus,
    is heard both loud and long.

And none dare listen, when the full moon glistens,
    upon the trees at night.
And any there, who have a care,
    for precious life take flight.

Strange deeds are done when the midnight sun,
    shines down upon the valley.
Dark, gory sights, in the darkest nights,
    as the Hordes of Hell there rally.

If any care listen, when the full moon glistens,
    they'll hear it if they wander.
A Hellish sound—fierce and around,
    beyond the green hills yonder.

But who can say in the pale of day,
    if these tales be false or true?
For none return, where the mountain burns,
    and bid their lives, "Adieu."

II

'Though he does what he can, what kills a man,
    is a lack of love and affection.
No use to explain and less to complain;
    no profit in disaffection.
Threescore years and ten, is the lot of men,
    so use them wisely I say.
We all must account, when at last we dismount,
    before God's Throne, some day.

I paid no heed, to other men's greed,
    and worked on in the fields.
Daily I wrought, good life I bought,
    to avarice I would not yield.

Each day I toiled, with the earth's good soil,
    and blessed the food I ate.
Each night I slept, wherein there crept,
    sweet dreams of my due fate.

No ambition had I, that I might try,
    to leave my parental home.
Save for the day, when my father away,
    and I was left alone.

Always I knew, when the cool breeze blew,
    I should be content with life.
'Till came that day, I dare hardly say,
    that caused me so much strife.

When my father left home, the hills to roam,
    I dared not say a word.
When mother saw him leave, her bosoms heaved,
    and her scream was all I heard.

But he never turned back as the day turned black;
    the sun set fast that night.
When I slept it seems, my every dream,
    was wracked with ghoulish sights.

The very next day, my mother did say,
    that father was gone for good.
'Till then her boy was her precious joy.
    Then slowly changed her mood.

As the days went by and before my eyes,
    my mother's demeanour changed.
No more laughter, heard I thereafter;
    she was as one deranged.

Silent she became; I thought her insane,
    as she looked at me with suspicion.
So I kept alone, within my home;
    safety lay in submission.

One morn I awoke, as the sun's light broke,
    upon my solitary home.
My door fast closed, against its host,
    as I slept there all alone.

Then I heard a crash, as my door fell fast,
    my mother stood in its frame.
Her hair awry, I did all but cry,
    as she cursed dear father's name.

A knife in her hand; I had not planned,
    I relied on the Good Lord's Grace.
She grabbed my throat, the knife she brought,
    down towards my face.

I screamed aloud, as she howled and howled.
    I turned and threw her o'er.
Still screaming loud, she cursed and scowled,
    as she sprung up from the floor.

But quick I dashed as on the bed she crashed.
    I ran fast from that house.
In fear for my life, escaping her knife,
    I ran from my father's spouse.

And I never looked back, at her attack,
    as I ran for all my life.
'Till breath I lacked, I fell on my back,
    safe from my father's wife.

But clothes I'd few, so when body renewed,
    I stood upon my feet.
As I looked around, some berries I found,
    that I might readily eat.

I had my fill and when hunger killed,
    I walked along the road.
In time I arrived at a town outside,
    and there I made my abode.

I slept in the streets, I rare did eat;
    I worked whenever I could.
And all the while, across distant miles,
    I felt the call of the woods.

At night I heard, strange whispered words,
carried upon the breeze.
Something called me from across a sea,
of forest, trees and leaves.

For weeks I heard unspeakable words,
as I recalled my mother's screams.
My worst nightmares were of my mother's stare,
as she haunted all my dreams.

So I made my mind, dear father to find,
in Hell's great Mountain tall.
And so at last, put to the past,
those hideous, Hellish bawls.

So I bought a horse, tall and coarse,
and then I bought a gun.
In the quiet of night, far from the light,
my deed was then soon done.

Away I went, on adventure bent,
I rode long into the dark.
And all too soon, beneath the shining moon,
I heard some wild dogs bark.

As a thief in the night, with all my might,
I rode towards the hills.
And ever I heard, my mother's words,
bending my mind and will.

Yet on I rode, to a distant abode,
    in the forest green and dark.
And safe at last, in the woodland dark,
    the dogs no longer barked.

But yet I feared, the darkness near,
    so I lit a fire and sat.
The flickering flames seemed to curse my name,
    as I waited in the dark.

No sleep had I, 'neath that woodland sky,
    for my body was wracked in pain.
As the daylight broke, to the dawn I spoke,
    and stood a man again.

The stars now gone and arose the sun,
    restoring my sense of might.
So quick I shook, the dark forsook,
    and rid me of the night.

Then on I rode, from my forest abode,
    I was glad to see the blue
of the day, as I made my way,
    for my courage was then renewed.

By the end of the day, I scarce could say,
    from whence I had come.
The forest thick, my mind played tricks,
    as down then sank the sun.

Then the man in me, he fast did flee,
    as the night came once again.
Left in the wild, like a fearful child,
    I thought I heard some men.

Quick down I fell for I fast would tell,
    what those voices said.
But my heart beat fast, for my soul aghast,
    it was the speech of the dead!

My horse then reared, for he too feared,
    and raced into the night.
And left alone, chilled to the bone,
    I prayed with all my might.

III

Dark tales are told of the river of gold,
    high on the Mountain trail.
And none return, from where it burns -
    so go the old men's tales.
And all who listen, have faces wizened;
    they rarely sleep that night.
The story that's told of the Mountain's gold,
    robs them of their might.

How I strained my ears as I tried to hear,
what those voices said.
And 'though I tried, I strained and sighed;
so cold I was half-dead.

The night wind blew, it cut me through,
I thought I'd die of cold.
And so I bemoaned, my time alone;
I'd never see the Mountain of Gold.

'Though trembling with fear, I was wont to hear,
the words of those whispered voices.
But the wind blew hard, I was driven half-mad.
Perchance they were but noises?

As I clutched my coat, fear gripped my throat.
Slowly I made my way,
to where the voices spoke, as a storm then broke!
And dawned a brand new day.

And as the sun arose, I no more froze,
but bathed in golden light.
On the forest ground, there I found,
I had but slept the night.

'Twas only a dream, it was clear it seemed,
so I woke once more a man.
But my body ached, as I did wake,
and then I felt a hand!

IV

They say that trail, is bleak and pale,
    for only the foolish go there.
But if you do, I'll tell you true,
    your bones will be picked bare.
There's naught but death to catch your breath,
    upon the Mountain of Gold.
But you'll come to harm and never be warm;
    you'll die of the bloody cold.

Soft and clean, so gentle it seemed,
	that touch was Heaven sent.
As I looked to see, where I might be,
	I knew not what it meant.

A dream I thought, of magic wrought,
	I never had dreamed so well.
When a voice I heard, like a woodland bird,
	in that fairy, woodland dell.

Up then I rose, from my fitful dose,
	and saw a maiden so fair,
that I faint would die, to Heaven fly,
	amongst the Angels there.

Her face did shine as she looked at mine;
	my heart was all a tremble.
And as she stood, in that sunlit wood,
	an Angel she resembled.

Her sweet, sweet scent, did circumvent,
	disquiet in my mind.
I scarce could speak, some meaning seek,
	in words that I might find.

She looked and smiled, I was quite beguiled;
	she held me in a trance.
I searched for words that I might be heard,
	in that happy, happenstance.

"Come rest by me," whispered she,
and led me by my hand,
to a glowing tent, where I then spent,
the day in comfort grand.

No task too small, that I recall;
she did all that I desired.
Good wine and food, I felt renewed,
sitting by her warm camp-fire.

As the sun went down, lying on the ground,
she turned to me and asked,
"What brought you here, pray lie me near,
what is your avowed task?"

She stroked my hair, her scent so fair,
I lay as 'though in dream.
Her voice so sweet, there would I keep,
so happy I was it seemed.

I closed my eyes and prayed on high,
my body now revived.
Far, far away, it seemed that day,
of fear I was deprived.

The singing birds, were all I heard,
as I lay there quite serene.
My eyes closed fast, once more she asked,
In that forest of verdant green.

So I looked at her, as a thought occurred,
    I sat up then and said,
"Ask not this but give your kiss.
    Let's be happy here instead.

"Let us these days, our fortunes praise,
    enjoy the forest's peace."
For troubles none, my fear undone,
    all terror now did cease.

Then she looked away, as if to say,
    she did not wish to hear.
Those words I said, rang in her head.
    When I looked she disappeared!

As I looked around, I heard a sound,
    like the rushing of the wind.
Then the sky turned dark, wild dogs barked,
    and cold became my skin.

Somewhere away, a voice did say,
    that I would surely die.
To a tree I clung, as the cold wind sang,
    and tears stung my eyes.

Away blew the tent, o'er the ground rent,
    and still the wind blew on.
Lightening streaked, my legs grew weak,
    and then the sun was gone!

Through the rain's hard blast, I held steadfast,
and weathered that awful night.
As the morning dawned, the horizon beyond,
I beheld a wondrous sight.

A rainbow grand, the sky now spanned,
and the wind fell to a breeze.
Thus I fell to ground, without a sound,
among the forest's leaves.

So sound I slept, in dreams I kept,
all the fears of that storm.
But when I awoke, my head was stroked,
by a scented hand so warm.

It was that Lady once more and again she wore,
a dress of silken green.
Her face shone bright in the morning light;
the most beautiful I had seen.

So startled I, beneath the forest sky,
I was dazed and so confused.
To my questions then, that I asked again,
to answer she refused.

I knew not why, she began to cry,
I begged sincere forgiveness.
But if she would keep, on and on to weep,
I would be about my business!

She dried her tears, face filled with fear,
    I saw her downcast gaze.
But she said no word, that I then heard,
    so I took to the forest maze.

I made my way, throughout that day,
    onward toward the gold.
With every step, o'er the ground I crept,
    now ever feeling bold.

V

Strange tales are told of the Mountain of Gold,
    by men who say they know,
where great riches lie, beneath the sky,
    whence a golden river flows.
'Though many do hear, those stories clear,
    they fear the silent voice,
that echoes in their heads, with fearful dread,
    that they never again rejoice.

So many days, upon that way,
    I walked and walked and walked.
With no company, to hear or see,
    there was no use to talk.

So I reflected then, on the many men,
    I had met in all my life.
So glad was I, 'neath the azure sky,
    that yet I had no wife.

For to me it seemed, that women schemed,
    so in them I placed no trust.
They had no thought for any or aught;
    some filled me with utter disgust.

Yet for all that and their idle chitchat,
    like the Lady in Forrest Green -
a delight was one, all said and done,
    The most lovely I had seen.

But even she, had abandoned me,
    and I could bare understand,
why she had cried, heaved and sighed,
    in that pleasant, wooded land.

So sweet her scent, I might gladly relent,
    my thoughts of that sex.
But as my mother's face, my memory graced,
    I thought of them the less.

Thus as I trod, on soil and clod,
    a lake I happened on.
And there I made, beside that glade,
    my shelter from the sun.

As on my way, my fears allayed,
    by that scene so calm and clear.
As I thought on he, whom I would see,
    I felt someone draw near.

VI

They say the tales, of the Northern trails,
    are told by only those
who have not seen, the cold, bleak scene,
    where flesh and bone froze.
The darkest days and the winding ways,
    are all that there remain.
Where howling gales, like the sharpest nails,
    blow round that snowy plain.

Upon the breeze, came through the leaves,
  of verdant colors bright,
it was there I saw, like never before,
  I bare believed my sight!

A brilliant glow, from high to low,
  I fell and covered my eyes.
Then came a sound from above the ground,
  that I should make reply.

"Why lie so low, on the ground below?"
  The voice was so sincere,
when I looked again, bare half a man,
  I saw a maiden clear.

It was the Lady in Green, whom I had seen,
  bare some days ago.
At me she smiled, once more beguiled,
  lying on the ground below.

Then I stood tall, as I heard her call,
  her beauty so clearly shone.
But as before, I placed no store:
  soon she might be gone!

But I greeted her, as I interred,
  my doubts and fears put aside.
I smiled to see, the greenery,
  and the mare by her side.

Smiling said I, as I caught her eye,
    "I see we meet once more.
What cause have you, why tell me true,
    to haunt me on this shore?

"The last we met, you did frown and fret,
    and now I see you here.
What cause have I, pray tell me why,
    that you should so appear?"

She looked up at me, that I might see,
    the smile upon her face.
But oh my heart! It would not start,
    there in that woodland place.

Her beauty shone, the glade upon,
    I near was dead with love.
For her scent came by and oh! but I,
    was like in Heaven above.

She approached me then, in that verdant glen,
    her beauty quite, quite serene.
Her perfumed hair, glistened there,
    in that green and pleasant scene.

"Let us converse . . . a while rehearse,
    what fears lie in your heart.
And then perchance, in this great expanse,
    our journey together start."

These words she spoke as on we talked,
    I could not look away.
Her face glowed clear, I moved to hear,
    her voice rose in a sway.

And she told me then of the many men,
    who ventured to the Mount of Gold.
Their souls ne'er returned, for in Hell they burned,
    while their bodies lay stiff with cold.

Intently I listened, in her bewitching prison,
    'though I scarce believed it so.
For I had no thought, of Hell or aught,
    or anything she did know.

There was no Devil, in Hell or Heaven;
    these were but children's tales.
But there I stayed, in that woodland glade,
    somewhere on the Mountain trail.

For all my adventures, I would scarce censure,
    the account she gave to me,
of hideous ghouls, in bloodied pools,
    and intolerable purgatory.

But tales I thought, were by ignorance brought,
    and not for me or mine.
Still I felt secure, with this Lady demure,
    in that wood of towering pine.

How many days, I cannot say,
    we passed those Halcyon days.
For naught I lacked, on that woodland track,
    and the time did fly away.

The best of wine, was hers and mine,
    as we camped out on that track.
I was ever treated, for she never depleted,
    her mare's limitless pack.

'Though I asked her then, 'twas beyond my ken,
    to know how could that be.
So I asked no more, of her unbounded store,
    so happy she had made me.

I asked her not, from whence she brought,
    such goodly food and wine.
I prayed I be, as happy as she,
    so great the juice of the vine.

The days went by, the nights did fly;
    I grew fat from my indolence.
We talked and sighed, we laughed and cried,
    I was in a state of ignorance.

Her kisses were sweet, when we would meet,
    in each other's warm embrace.
Such utter delight, each day and night,
    I luxuriated in her good grace.

And yet and yet, whenever we met,
    in love's nocturnal bliss,
'though her skin was soft and I lacked for naught,
    and yearned for her hungry kiss.

Yet something was missing, in this my prison;
    I could not clearly see.
The indolent life, was causing me strife,
    it would not let me be.

For I never could tell, in that luxuriant dell,
    whence came such food and wine.
Her dark mare's pack, like a mighty sac—
    it seemed never to decline!

When it I approached, or the subject broached,
    she took me fast aside.
So it remained then, far beyond my ken;
    that knowledge I was denied.

So, fool that I was, it served my cause,
    to remain with her those days.
I near forgot, what I had sought –
    to travel the Mountain way.

So lost was I, I bare did try,
    to remember my dear lost father.
With her to stay, then and always,
    I would then much rather.

Then dark one night, by the moon's pale light,
    I woke and she had gone!
And in her stead, alone in my bed,
    quickly approached the dawn.

There was her pack, that mysterious sac,
    that was me long denied.
As I looked on it, dare I permit,
    to boldly look inside?

Outside I looked, by a bubbling brook;
    no sight of her saw I.
Then back I went inside the tent,
    I felt near like to die.

But then I supposed, I should pity those,
    who were not free as I.
And smiling again, merry countenance feigned,
    I looked up at the sky.

The sun shone bright, as it's rays of light,
    pierced right down to the ground.
I gathered the tent and before I went,
    I took one last look around.

And to my surprise, right before my eyes,
    a mule wandered close by.
So, "Right," says I, before it went by,
    "You can help me now to fly."

So I roped it there and with great care,
    I packed the tent on its back.
And before I departed, for the Mountain started,
    I picked up the Lady's pack.

Then on I trod, along that woodland road;
    I never did look behind.
For the past was past and the future at last,
    was what I sought to find.

VII

It's often been told, that the Mountain of Gold,
　　is not meant for any of us.
And the fools who dare, to venture there,
　　are rarely in company discussed.
And those who wish, the gold to kiss,
　　find more than they can spend.
But their heart's desire, leads to Hell's fire;
　　that's where they meet their end.

After two more days, along that way,
    I found a meadow green.
I almost forgot, what I had lost,
    and the places I had been.

Then I pitched the tent and a night I spent,
    beneath a starry sky.
And I woke at dawn, the following morn,
    with sleep still in my eyes.

I washed my face and cast my gaze,
    to where the Mountain lay.
It's snow cast peak, did seem to speak,
    of treasure hidden away.

As the snow glistened, intently I listened,
    and imagined what might be.
It's song I heard, it's every word,
    was speaking only to me.

That song so sweet, I could barely keep,
    from singing in my heart.
In that pleasant scene, that meadow green,
    I once again did start.

That mule and I, did by and by,
    walked ever on and on.
We walked all day in that meadow gay,
    beneath the clouds and sun.

But alas! Alas! My food flew fast,
    and water had I none!
And to now go back, for the food I lacked,
    was like in Hell to burn.

To now retreat, was a greater feat,
    than my poor heart could bear.
So on I went, 'though my food was spent,
    through that meadow fair.

I slapped the mule, like the bloody fool,
    that I had always been.
My foolish quest, laid me to rest,
    in that meadow of deep, deep green.

But my hand fast fell, in that lush, green dell,
    upon the Lady's pack.
For something inside, from me did hide,
    lying on the mule's back.

So I took it down and on the ground,
    I laid it by my feet.
The mule stood there (I forsook its stare),
    I wished so much to eat.

What might be there? I must beware,
    perhaps some queer device?
But inside I knew, whence came the brew,
    in that verdant paradise.

So cautiously, I looked to see,
    the contents of that sac.
And before my eyes, to my surprise,
    a feast lay in that pack!

Inside I saw, food rare and raw,
    as befits a Royal table.
Like a starving beast, upon that feast,
    I fast ate as I was able.

I drank the wine, ate food so fine,
    that soon I was revived.
I took my fill and yet it still,
    more food for me devised!

It emptied not, so on that spot,
    I fell into deepest slumber.
I dreamed such dreams, of valleys and streams,
    and my Mountain's waiting plunder.

When sleep left me, I bare could see,
    for Night had cast a veil,
upon all the ground, that lay around,
    far on the Mountain trail.

There was all but black, in that Hellish dark;
    there was but one faint light,
coming from the pack, the Lady's sac,
    in that dark and dismal night.

I sat in awe, at what I saw,
as I approached and looked inside.
A low, soft glow, was there below,
as my eyes then opened wide.

For the brightest sun, the night undone,
shot forth from in that pack.
I was thrown aside, by that bag beside,
as it lit the Mountain track.

No more cold and once more bold,
I lifted it on high.
There never was light as on that night,
so welcome to my eyes.

Full rested then, I rose again,
and continued on my way.
So I walked all night, by that strange, bright light,
until there came the day.

And as the morn, shone with the dawn,
came hunger pangs once more.
It's light now dimmed, I held it still,
the pack had food galore!

I wolfed it down, with ravenous sounds,
I ate 'till I was filled.
I drank the wine and when I had dined,
my hunger was completely stilled.

Then rested I, beneath that sky,
    my dreams were calm and free.
The Lady in Green whom I had seen,
    in dreams, she spoke to me.

But I never did hear, her words unclear,
    yet I smelled her blossomed scent.
And so it remained as my journey regained,
    to my Mountain I once more went.

Throughout that day, I dare now say,
    as I walked the Mountain trail,
my mind was filled, with that vision still,
    of my mother's hideous wail.

What caused her change, her mind derange?
    I thought on it so long,
that I quite forgot, what I had sought,
    as I went that trail along.

Then came the night, fast went the light,
    I made to settle down.
The moon rose high, in the blackened sky,
    I recalled my father's frown.

Our last embrace and his sorrowful face,
    as he left our home that day.
He told me then, as those other men,
    he'd be on the Mountain way.

As I closed my eyes, beneath that silent sky,
I wished my father well.
Wherever he was, whatever his cause,
in Heaven or that Mountain Hell.

My mother too, my thoughts renewed,
for her I felt some guilt.
How would she be, as one not three,
in the house my father built?

As the cold night bit, my teeth I grit,
and pulled my blanket tight.
As on the ground, I lay around,
surrounded by stars that night.

The cold bit through, my misery renewed,
I cursed my threadbare clothes.
But no use to curse, for better or worse,
my eyes were near to close.

VIII

When the cold stars glisten, if you care to listen,
    you might hear the voice of God.
Yet the Mountain trail, so goes the tale,
    is paved with frozen clod.
And if you care and if you dare,
    to walk that deathly way,
you'll meet the dead, as on they tread –
    Well . . . at least that's what they say.

I thought to freeze, my heart to seize,
    and die that very night.
And never again, like those foolish men,
    enjoy the day's sunlight.

So I cursed aloud, in my blanket shroud;
    I shouted loud and long.
As I turned around, lying on the ground,
    I thought I heard a song.

It was only the howl, some nocturnal fowl,
    as it mocked me far away.
The sound cut deep and stole my sleep,
    along the Mountain way.

Far in the night, far from the light,
    I thought I'd die of cold.
I near gave up, on life's full cup,
    when I saw a light of gold.

The Lady's pack, lay on that track,
    a soft glow from it came.
Oh that Lady in Green, in that woodland scene,
    who set my heart aflame.

Out stretched my hand in that frozen land,
    toward that pack aglow.
And there I found, on the frozen ground,
    a blanket in the snow.

Quick up I stood, in better mood,
I swathed my body in it.
I bare did blink, beneath that sky of ink,
so warm I felt within it.

So I laughed out loud, beneath the clouds,
I jumped and danced with glee.
So warm I felt, as the snow did melt,
I slept so calm and free.

'Though the wind screamed, lost in my dreams,
I passed that fitful night.
I dreamt I saw, in a vision of awe,
that Lady dressed in light.

Like a Summer sky, was the light in her eyes;
she smelled like a garden of flowers.
To me it seemed as on I dreamed,
I walked in a Heavenly bower.

I feared to wake, that path to take;
I did all to keep that dream.
That Lady in Green, to me she seemed,
like womanhood supreme.

But I must rise and open my eyes,
and continue upon my way.
So up I rose, where once was snow,
as the sun rose on that day.

IX

I've heard it said, that only the dead,
    walk on the Mountain trail.
And only the wise, to all advise,
    take heed of their warning tale.
When winds blow high, beneath the Mountain sky,
    I implore you all to listen.
For if we do (and I'm told it's true),
    we'll escape the Mountain's prison.

So I journeyed on, as the glorious dawn,
    turned into noon-day high.
And far ahead, I thought the dead,
    lay beneath the sapphire sky,

I saw the cap, of the Mountain trap,
    beckon to do my worst.
As the hours wore on and the day near done,
    I began once more to thirst.

In the evening air, a sound so fair,
    seemed to come from the Mountain top.
Like a pleasant song, it willed me along;
    I walked with no will to stop.

But my thirst grew strong, as I traveled along;
    I reached for my supply of water.
But it was all gone, like the dipping sun,
    when I heard the forest's daughter.

The Lady in Green, to me it seemed,
    was calling me in song.
'Though water denied, I thought I spied,
    as that trail I went along.

Some vision or scene, like in my dream,
    of that maiden with such face,
as to drive me mad, to my burdens add.
    I prayed God grant me grace.

My throat so dry beneath a darkening sky,
    and still the song went on.
Yet still that trail, before me hailed,
    continue 'till light was gone.

So on I trod, on that wearisome road,
    as my thirst grew ever strong.
Then the evening birds, on high I heard,
    and saw them depart in throngs.

As the sun went away at the end of the day,
    I made as if to bed.
How I wished I had—it drove me half-mad!—
    some water and some bread.

I arranged a space, in that lonesome place;
    I happened to reach for the pack.
So heavy it was and all because,
    more food lay in that sac!

But I'd eaten it all (I was quite enthralled),
    the night before for sure.
So I ate and drank, to God gave thanks,
    my hunger and thirst quite cured.

As Night cast her pall, over us all,
    and the stars faded one by one,
for light I cried, 'else I had died,
    such solitude I did shun.

From the pack then fell, something I could tell,
	I turned and felt in the dark.
A candle in hand, in all that land!
	And yet I had no spark!

As flint I had none! Once more undone!
	I cursed my luckless fate.
As I closed my eyes and prayed to the skies,
	my foolishness full berate.

As I opened my eyes, my sight did belie,
	for the candle now was lit!
It's light fell around upon the ground,
	from it's single, solitary wick!

How could this be? It was beyond me,
	to understand any or aught!
Were some company, bewitching me?
	It was my only thought.

But candle in hand, I searched the land:
	no sign of any other men.
I dropped the thought, that confusion wrought,
	and turned to sleep again.

As I drifted to sleep, I hoped to keep,
	a night in fitful dreams,
of that Lady in Green, for to me she seemed,
	a veritable, woodland Queen.

Having eaten well, a chiming bell,
  did haunt my sleep that night.
Of that Lady true, I had not a clue,
  until the morning light.

The sun did brake, bade me awake,
  and continue on my quest.
So I traveled on, that trail upon,
  until at night came rest.

But all day long, I heard the song,
  she sang by the woodland stream.
That sweet melody, had haunted me,
  as she did in my dreams.

But a bell now chimed, in fearful time,
  whenever I thought on her.
Like some deathly march or black-death barge,
  and the mortal smell of myrrh.

But I cast away my fears that day,
  I preferred to think good thoughts.
As I lay me down, upon the ground,
  I considered all I'd lost.

My house, my home—and now alone,
  I wandered on this road.
And my father dear, near half a year,
  as onward now I trod.

X

I know it's said, that only the dead,
would follow the Mountain road.
For the Devil they say, has hidden away,
his gold in his Mountain abode.
And only a fool, confronts the ghouls,
that guard his precious treasure.
And if you dare, to travel there,
you'll remain at his eternal pleasure.

So many days, along that way,
    I wandered all but lost.
In blistering heat, through snow and sleet,
    in rain, hail and frost.

But that mule and I, we ever did try,
    towards that Mountain tall.
But the mule grew old, on the trail so cold,
    and eventually it did fall.

That stupid mule—and I the fool!
    who'd bought and lost a horse!
We both would die and know not why.
    I cried 'till I was hoarse.

The mule laid down and with fearful frown,
    I cursed him to the sky.
He faced his death and with a final breath,
    he finally closed his eyes.

No use to curse, to scream or worse;
    he'd finally found some rest.
I thought that I would also die.
    He'd given of his best.

So I gathered my goods, as well I could,
    and left him there to rot.
And on my way, for the rest of the day,
    that mule I soon forgot.

With every step, as on I crept,
  a mighty mare I wished.
Like that Lady's horse, I wished of course,
  but she it seemed had vanished.

No sooner wished, fortune me kissed,
  I bare believed my eyes!
I heard a neigh, on the Mountain way;
  a horse was my great prize.

I dropped my goods and there she stood,
  I rubbed my eyes once more.
A great black mare, before me there!
  Oh! How my heart did soar.

I bare believed, I hardly conceived,
  how could this possibly be?
In that wilderness, I quick acquiesced,
  and called that mare to me.

And quick she came, I grabbed her mane,
  she was tall, strong and tame.
So gracefully, she did come to me,
  but what could be her name?

But saddle none! Again undone!
  I cursed my poor, ill-fortune!
Nor any rein, never mind a name;
  and soon up rose the moon.

So I laid me down, upon the ground,
    I thought to sleep that night.
The saddle bag, I picked and dragged;
    it glowed like soft moonlight.

Inside I saw, within that glow,
    a whiskey bottle full.
I took a sip and on my lips,
    it tasted smooth and cool.

XI

I've heard many tales of the Mountain trail,
        and how it traps men's souls.
Their hunger and lust, for the glittering dust,
        drives them to that goal.
But when they arrive, to escape they strive,
        but futility is all they find.
But no matter then, those poor, fool men;
        it's gold that makes them blind.

I felt the sun when the night was done;
   the mare stood by my bed.
As in sunlight bathed, I was fair amazed -
   A saddle beneath my head!

And by my bed, near to my head,
   lay a bridle and a bit.
How could this be? Lying there by me,
   Was a complete rider's kit!

But the night before, I had implored,
   Great God for just that!
There were none then, when I said, "Amen."
   If wrong, I'd eat my hat!

So sure I was of that because,
   I knew I'd searched around.
No saddle or rein, I thought again,
   I knew I had not found.

And yet . . . and yet, my mind beset,
   such questions did abound.
There was no doubt, the saddle about,
   before me on the ground.

No-one in sight, with whom I might,
   discuss this mystery.
As none laid claim, to my vanishing shame,
   I claimed it all for me.

The saddle's construction, was finest production,
the best I'd ever seen.
The finest leather, there was no better;
fit for a Woodland Queen.

Then on I strode, along that road,
towards the Mountain high.
I whistled a tune and very soon,
I came a streamlet by.

A pleasant glade and so I made,
to spend some time in rest.
The water I drank and God I thanked,
such fortune—I was blessed.

As I rested there, amidst forest air,
I sat against a tree.
In waking dreams, to me it seemed,
the mare tugged at my knee.

Eyes open wide, that stream beside,
I heard a noise somewhere.
Alert again, I heard some men -
I said a silent prayer.

I reached for my gun; around I spun;
a man and horses two.
He raised his arms all alarmed,
to show me he was true.

"Whoa! Whoa," he cried, his pistol I spied.
"Take care what you do with that gun.
I've not many years, left to live I fear,
But I'd like to live them, son."

"Drop the pistol," I said, a voice in my head,
told me he was no good.
He dismounted his steed and we both agreed,
we'd share some drink and food.

He was agèd and bent, an elderly gent;
his hair was long and white.
His wrinkled skin and speech wherein,
he was so calm and polite.

He thanked me fine, for the food and wine;
he never had dined so well.
Gentry he seemed, he smiled and beamed,
his story he wished to tell.

As he sat by my fire, I came to admire,
this man who seemed so serene.
Intently I listened, for his eyes like a prism,
transformed the woodland scene.

He had travelled these days, from far away;
near the Mountain his partner had left.
When he woke with the dawn, early one morn,
of his partner he was bereft.

'Though he made a search, his horse lurched,
    and he never did find his man.
But screaming he heard—and Devilish words;
    his homeward journey began.

XII

When the moon shines bright on the Mountain at night,
    it's said the gold shines too.
And when the frost glistens, wild dogs listen,
    for the Devil and his Hellish crew.
For it's then they say, before the break of day,
    they'll claim at least one soul.
And in a Hellish prison with nightmare visions,
    it'll rue it's love of gold.

When his story was told, I asked of the gold.
Had he seen it? I asked him then.
But he looked away and would not say,
so I asked him once again.

Then he looked at me, so fearfully,
he seemed so much in pain.
Had he seen the gold? I would be told,
so I asked him once again.

But his speech seemed lost and like a ghost,
he stared into the distance.
I thought I spied, a tear in his eye,
as he broke out of his trance.

"Listen good my son, you'll be undone,
if you ever should go out there.
Leave it alone. Go on! Go home.
Ride back on your lovely mare."

I would not be told, I wanted the gold,
pointing my pistol at him.
"Tell me true, or sure I'll kill you,"
I told him once again.

"No use to say that," as he picked up his hat,
"I don't want to spoil your sleep.
So I'll bid you good-day and be on my way,
I'd rather your soul, you keep.

"Take it from me, you never want to see,
    the sights that met these eyes.
So be just like me, I beg, let it be,
    for it's exceedingly good advice."

But I wanted to know, for him to show,
    how I might venture there.
I wanted the gold, I'd not be told,
    I was deaf to his words so fair.

"Old man say this," at him I hissed,
    through teeth hard-clenched in disgust.
"What made you a coward,"—the forest I scoured.
    "Why should I you now trust?

"You've eaten my food, that tasted so good,
    you've drunk my whiskey and wine.
It's little to ask, some aid with my task,
    and then you can go just fine.

"So tell me now, just tell me how,
    I can reach the Mountain of Gold.
Just tell me this, or it'll be remiss,
    if your story isn't told."

"Listen son," said he, "just let it be,
    and you'll have many tales to tell.
Let's part company, just you and me,
    you don't wanna go to Hell."

But I'd not be denied; as I looked in his eyes,
I knew to heed him well.
Truth, plain to see, he was telling to me.
From somewhere there chimed a bell!

In his eyes was fear. He dried his tears,
that man now bent and old.
If he ever knew what, of any or aught,
he did not want the gold.

"I know you can hear," he said with fear.
"That bell you've heard it before.
Now I can tell, for I know this real well,
it summons you to Hell's door.

"So leave this damned place, or in utter disgrace,
you'll be the Devil's prey.
Please let it be! Please come with me,
or you'll never see the light of day.

"For the food I'll pay and be on my way.
You're most welcome to come along.
If you cannot trust, an old man, I must,
take my leave and now go home."

"It's you I don't trust," I hissed and I cursed.
"You can't just leave and go home!
I want that gold and I will be told,
even if I go alone."

"Take it from me," the old man said he,
"you'll thank me well some day.
When you've a wife, a child and happy life,
you'll be glad you did not stay.

"So, thank you again, 'though it causes me pain,
to see you hunger for gold.
If you go to the Mount, it's bodies you'll count,
and die, for it's Hellish cold."

"No! I'll kill you before," I cursed and I swore,
at that poor man standing there.
"I'll not tell you again, I'll kill you and then,
I'll leave without a care."

"No, you won't do that and you won't grow fat,
if gold is your heart's desire.
If that's what you want, you'll end up gaunt,
burning in Hell's hot fires.

"So listen to me son, the day's near done,
and I'll leave or soon go to sleep.
If it's gold that you wish, I'll give you this,
it's all yours for to keep."

From his pocket he took, as on I looked,
a small purse of leather and string.
Inside there was gold, so hard and so cold,
when I heard the distant bell ring.

"Aye, I hear it too, it's a bitter, bitter brew,
 that sound for to drink.
Son pay it no cause, I beg you because,
 it's far, far worse than you think.

"That bell called those, who now are froze,
 somewhere inside that rock.
If you'll listen to me, we'll both of us flee,
 afore Lucifer runs amok."

I laughed out loud, as I imagined a crowd,
 of poor and foolish old men,
all rotting away, awaiting Doomsday.
 I laughed all the more again.

"That's a mighty fine story, I'll give you the glory,
 you've kept me entertained for a while.
But it's time to speak true, so I'm asking for you,
 to take me these last few miles."

"I'll not freely go there, for foul or fair,
 nor all the gold on earth.
For none return, in Hell they burn.
 My life is far more worth.

"I see you won't stop, you're determined to drop,
 into the fires of Hell.
So I'll take my leave, for I cannot achieve,
 to dissuade you, I can tell.

"You're heading for Hell, as I can tell,
    your life will soon be undone.
But even worse, you'll ever be cursed,
    in fires hotter than the sun.

"My honour to retain, I'll tell you again,
    give up this foolish quest.
Come home with me and forever be free,
    and give yourself some rest.

"I see you're still young, too young for a gun,
    but you're no killer I well guess.
So leave it alone, go on! Go home,
    and be a man no less.

"It pains me to tell but now that the bell,
    has rung and we heard it alright.
My partner's my son, whose soul is undone,
    in the Devil's eternal night.

"So I'm going to go—you can't tell me, 'No!'
    I'll pray for you going home.
But please take this knife, it may save your life,
    if you're going to go alone."

As he walked toward me, I could plainly see,
    a knife in his right hand.
But there was none before! Of that I was sure,
    as he walked to me on the land.

I knew not his intent, so a bullet I sent.
    I pulled my trigger and fell.
He stopped in his track, bullet hit the mark;
    he dropped among the bluebells.

The look on his face, in that woodland place,
    I recall it so clearly still.
The look of surprise he had in his eyes;
    I had the poor man killed!

As he fell to his knees, amongst the trees,
    his knife fell to the ground.
Then he fell to his side, I knew he had died,
    he departed without a sound.

Suddenly I found, lying on the ground,
    something awful inside.
I heaved aloud, beneath the scudding clouds,
    and vomited the stream beside.

Lord I felt so ill, that the man I'd killed;
    he lay still on the leaves.
I could hardly believe and began to grieve,
    when a scent came on the breeze.

The bluebells quivered and I felt a shiver,
    run down my spine right there.
There was something amiss, I was so sure of this,
    perhaps a wolf or a bear?

But quickly it passed, so again I cast,
    my eyes towards the old man.
Then I wept like child, for that old man mild,
    regretting my quest e'er began.

But the day turned dark, with only the sparks,
    of stars high up in the sky.
On the following morn, right after the dawn,
    I'd bury the man who'd died.

I gathered my bed and laid down my head,
    on the Lady's saddle pack.
I could not there sleep, in that woodland deep,
    so alone in the dark.

A gentle glow from the pack soon flowed,
    as I rested my head upon it.
Suddenly it seemed I was wrapped in dreams,
    of the Devil's fiery pit.

XIII

It's said that the cold, of the Mountain of Gold,
burns through to a man's bare bones.
For the love of treasure, grants no-one pleasure,
and you're bound to end up all alone.
And any who dare, to ever journey there,
they say are never the same.
For the Devil it's said, surrounded by the dead,
sits laughing in Hell's hot flames.

Perhaps it was right, deep in that night,
that I should suffer nightmares.
For that man I had killed, his life cut still,
I endured his deathly stare.

And 'though I screamed, it still did seem,
that none could hear my pain.
And if they did, from me they hid,
as I screamed again and again.

In the morning I heard, the stirring of birds,
as they flew about the sky.
I washed in the stream, put away my dreams,
when I saw a green butterfly.

I thought it strange, in that woodland range,
to see such a beautiful sight.
The scent of the flowers in that woodland bower,
dispelled my fear of the night.

I mounted the mare, in the woodland there,
and onward made my way.
And all too soon, beneath the shimmering moon,
I lay down at the end of the day.

But as the moon there shone, that land upon,
and I was troubled within.
Careless fool that I was! I cursed me because,
I'd committed another grave sin!

In that woodland bed, I'd left him for dead,
    I'd forgotten to bury the corpse!
That poor old man, who'd done me no harm,
    was there still with his horse.

But he was out of sight and late was the night,
    in my mind I'd never go back.
But I told myself so, that to bury him I'd go,
    and slept with my head on the pack.

But deep in my soul, I was troubled of old;
    that poor man's face I saw.
The look of surprise, he could not disguise,
    as my bullet there laid him low.

I told myself so, that the fatal blow,
    was none of my concern.
Why, if he was dead, laid in a cold bed,
    it was his folly not to learn.

Had I not told him so, that he was not to go,
    before I'd learned of the gold?
He'd have taken my life and with his knife,
    I'd be a body without a soul.

But the old man came back as I slept on the pack,
    he haunted my dreams that night.
His screaming son and the sound of my gun,
    made me crave the day's safe light.

At last I awoke, at the very first stroke,
of that hideous Devil bell.
It echoed in my head, like the screaming dead,
when a perfumed scent I smelled.

That calming scent was from Heaven sent,
the pain in my head soon died.
As I looked around, no-one I found,
I could not help but cry.

For beside my bed, were two gifts from the dead,
a knife and another purse of gold.
Had the old man come back? But yet no track!
The thought burned through to my soul.

Should I return? My quest adjourn?
Should I return to bury that man?
But in my head, I knew he was dead,
I'd not now abandon my plan.

But with shaking hand, I scanned the land;
there was no-one near me now.
Fearing for my life, I picked up the knife,
and gathered my courage somehow.

And the purse of gold, I placed in a fold,
in my shirt beneath my jacket.
I mounted the mare and fled from there,
safeguarding my leather packets.

XIV

I've heard many tales of the Mountain trail,
where the Devil walks here and there,
searching for souls to add to his gold,
so I bid you all beware.
I never have heard, a single, good word,
about that Devil, Auld Nick.
For I've often been told that men's love of gold,
he'll employ for them to trick.

The nights and the days, I spent on that way,
 they went without mishap.
But ever and on, that road upon,
 I travelled without a map.

Up and down hills, whether good or ill,
 I recalled the Green Lady's words.
An old man I'd killed, who haunted my will.
 Why? It seemed so absurd!

To think I had feared, such stories so weird,
 that could but frighten a child.
Why! I was no fool, to be frightened by ghouls!
 To my quest I was reconciled.

I lacked neither food, nor ever I could,
 for the Green Lady's saddle-pack,
'though light as feather and of the best leather,
 was filled like a grocer's sack.

And as for drink, I need hardly think,
 it was always in that sack.
In the darkest night, it provided me light,
 and banished oppressive dark.

And if I was cold, like a frosty old soul,
 it gave me a blanket of wool.
No more it surprised my eager eyes,
 'though light, it was ever full.

I took it for granted, that bag enchanted,
it held no wonder for me.
For what I admired, or ever desired,
it provided continually.

And so to the Mountain, that veritable fountain,
of eternal youth and treasure.
Closer it seemed, just as in my dreams,
the source of my greatest pleasure.

A few days I guessed, no more, no less,
and I would reach it's base.
And there would be, such gold for me,
in that happy, happy place.

XV

I once heard a lad, gave all that he had,
　　for a map to the Mountain trail.
But when he arrived, he was barely alive,
　　and never did tell his tale.
For the Devil they say, saw him that day,
　　and slowly removed his heart.
Then flew his soul, to the Mountain of Gold,
　　where his torment then did start.

I rode my mare without a care,
    and rode right to the rock.
Arriving at night, in the pale moonlight,
    in awe I was forced to stop.

Looking on high, to the night sky,
    the moon shone back and bright.
Behold! Behold! A river of gold!
    What a wondrous, wondrous sight!

I could never have planned by head or hand,
    the sight that I saw there.
A great waterfall, from that Mountain tall,
    my heart skipped beats I declare.

The moon's pale light, shining there bright,
    made it look like a river of gold.
I stood there in awe, of all that I saw,
    more beautiful than I'd been told.

But the moon rose fast and the light soon passed,
    as a cloud then covered it's face.
And only the stars, shimmering afar,
    gave light to that wondrous place.

Soon the river did seem, no more to gleam,
    and took an aura of doom.
It's crashing sound, rang all around,
    in that dark and dismal gloom.

But my Lady's sac, her magical pack,
    gave to me some warmth and light.
And so to bed, I laid my head,
    and slept throughout the night.

The morning soon, resounded to tunes,
    of birds as they took to flight.
I rose from my bed and shook my head,
    basking in the golden sunlight.

I was enjoying the air, while standing there,
    listening to the sound of the river.
I approached the water as the air turned hotter,
    where river was still like a mirror.

As I looked at my reflection, inspiring recollections,
    of days spent swimming at home.
That sense of belonging was an idle fool's yawning;
    I knew I was quite alone.

But no time for that, so I removed my hat,
    and washed my face in that pool.
The water was clear and filled me with cheer,
    it felt so inviting and cool.

To swim I gave thought, when something caught,
    my eye near to the river's edge.
And fluttering there, a butterfly fair,
    rose up to a Mountain ledge.

I saw it so clear, to me it appeared,
    as one I had seen before.
It's wings were so green, as before I had seen,
    like a Lady I once adored.

But I paid it no heed, for my immediate need,
    was to eat and have a drink.
So I returned to the mare, standing quietly there,
    beside the river's brink.

So then as I ate and quietly did wait,
    watching the river flow by.
I turned my mind to thoughts more refined,
    as I looked at the Mountain high.

And once again there, was that butterfly fair,
    and yet . . . I seemed to recall . . .
Yes! I suddenly recalled, those colors so bold,
    in a creature so beautifully small.

In that woodland bower, filled full with flowers,
    I smelled that scent once again.
But my mind I said, played tricks on my head -
    I was the most foolish of men.

My hunger and thirst, were quite dispersed,
    I had them both satisfied.
I put the saddle pack, upon the mare's back,
    to gold my mind I applied.

I explored that place, around the Mountain's base,
  I searched for the next three days.
But of gold no sign, that I could find,
  along that Mountain way.

And every day, along that way,
  I felt that I was not alone.
But none but I, walked beneath that sky,
  near to that Mountain stone.

So I closed my mind to what I might find,
  and searched for my heart's pleasure.
And every day, my thoughts strayed,
  considering the Mountain's treasure.

On the third day, along that way,
  the skies were rent apart.
Lightening flashed, for shelter I dashed,
  to still my beating heart.

The thunder roared and the rain poured;
  all around was sodden wet.
So dark the sky, the mare and I,
  with fear we were beset.

I ran for cover, where I discovered,
  just below the Mountain's face,
covered by brush, deep green and lush,
  a cave at the Mountain's base.

But the lightening struck, a bush I clutched,
as I fell into that cave.
The bush now alight, with fire so bright,
I was saved from a fiery grave.

But my horse was outside and ‘though I cried,
I heard her gallop away.
I was trapped inside, therein to hide,
from the dark, tempestuous day.

So I construed, there was naught to do,
but wait for the bush to die.
And ‘though I waited, the fire unabated,
I glimpsed what seemed a butterfly.

But I was distracted, by the fire protracted,
I simply could not understand.
Why the fire went on like a Summer’s sun,
yet did not consume the land.

I watched in awe, as I had before,
as the bush burned on and on.
There was no resolution and no conclusion.
When would the fire be done?

The cave was well lit, so I decided to sit,
as I could not leave and escape.
But now dry and warm, safe from the storm,
I was fully wide-awake.

But I realized then, that of all men,
    I was a fool and stupid to boot.
As I sat and stared, I knew my mare,
    had galloped away for good.

The hours passed by, I began to sigh,
    would that fire never burn out?
But the silence swallowed, my thoughts hollow,
    and so I did up and shout.

Off I threw, both my shoes,
    into the back of the cave.
And on feet now bare, I stood and stared,
    and vented my anger grave.

"What nightmare is this, that a bush can hiss,
    and crackle and burn and burn?
Yet never burn out, 'though I scream and shout,
    and never to home return!"

My voice echoed round, in alarming sound,
    and seemed to come from everywhere.
I covered my ears, in a fit of fear,
    collapsing and cowering there.

Like a mighty hall, majestic and tall,
    the Mountain did seem to reply.
From inside and out, it seemed to shout,
    that very soon I should die.

A voice filled with hate, where I must wait,
    had spoken to me of death.
As the noise died down, I rose from the ground,
    head ringing with labored breath.

There was none but I, that I could spy,
    in that Mountain prison.
And none to hear, my shouts of fear,
    none that would me listen.

The bush burned still, it was not killed,
    I thought to lose my mind.
Keen thought I gave, in that dismal cave,
    that escape I somehow find.

I was trapped I knew, so to bid adieu,
    to the Mountain I could never.
To burn in fire, like a funeral pyre,
    I would remain there ever and ever.

On bended knees, my anguished pleas,
    dissipated into the air.
What use to cry? I must surely die,
    inside that Mountain lair.

XVI

There are so many tales, of the Mountain trail,
    that one book can barely contain.
But is it for me, to sail that sea,
    which does all life drain?
So often it's said, that none but the dead,
    dare to walk that Mountain trail.
There's nothing to learn, where Hell's fires burn,
    save perhaps this sorry tale.

I was in despair, for none did care,
to hear my cries of woe.
I was all alone, in that place of stone;
to death I must now go.

So I stopped my tears and faced my fear;
I clasped my hands so tight.
In that place there, I resorted to prayer,
as the bush burned on so bright.

"I know my God, that You are Lord,
over all men and their souls.
It was foolish of me, my home to flee,
in search of the Mountain of Gold.

"I ask in this prayer, dear God so fair,
deliver me from this place.
I am yet young and slow of tongue.
Grant me Devine Grace."

I heard a noise! My heart rejoiced!
There was a God after all!
I turned to see, a man before me,
standing there, proud and tall.

"No point to pray, it's here you'll stay,"
he said from the back of the cave.
"Come with me, if you want to be free,
or stay here in your grave."

He was skinny and tall, standing near the wall,
 in shadow at the back of the cave.
He looked straight at me and I at he,
 in that dim, stony conclave.

"Come follow on, or you'll be undone,
 I know the way out of here.
Don't be a clown. Don't hang around!
 Don't be a slave to fear.

"That bush will burn, you'll never return,
 to the trail through that there way.
If you want to go home, don't stay here alone,
 I'll help and you'll get away."

But who are you? This can't be true,
 I thought within my mind.
Not a moment ago, this much I know,
 here, I alone was confined.

He flashed a smile and all the while,
 my mind was all perplexed.
A burning bush, that quite refused,
 to die—left me so vexed.

He smiled again and only then,
 I saw his tooth of gold.
It flashed so bright, it took my sight,
 and moments to regain control.

As he beckoned me, I bare believed,
    he disappeared from my view.
But then I saw, a gaping flaw,
    how could this be true?

I followed fast and soon we passed,
    inside the Mountain rock.
So fast I ran, following that man,
    he turned to me to talk.

My heart beat fast, then slowed at last,
    inside a great, empty space.
And there I spied, that man beside,
    a wonder in that place.

A river of gold, so bright and cold,
    lit the whole of that space.
But no crashing sound, did there resound,
    a mere whisper in that place.

For the waterfall, from that Mountain tall,
    flowed up from the ground!
I stood and stared at that marvel there,
    as confusion reigned all around.

And near the top, it did not stop,
    but disappeared into the stone.
How could this be? Perhaps sorcery?
    It chilled me to the bone.

"Come, sit by me for it's plain to see,
you do not believe your eyes.
Why think it strange? Come and exchange,
with me your reason why."

His speech was slow and seemed to flow,
before, behind and around me.
And in my head I thought he said,
"Now you'll never be free."

So slowly I walked as still he talked,
and again I saw him smile.
That flash of gold, shot through to my soul,
as I listened all the while.

But how did he sit? I had to admit,
I saw no seat or chair.
Yet his hips and knees, were bent with ease,
as he sat on only air.

"Who are you?" My confusion grew.
I approached with trepidation.
"What is your name?" I asked again,
as I watched his levitation.

I thought he laughed, as I considered his craft.
Was it illusion of some type?
It made no sense and in my defence,
I never had seen the like.

No wood or string, on which to swing,
could I see or discern.
Yet still I saw, with wonder and awe;
how would I ever learn?

"Suspend your thoughts, your mind and aught,
you have ever known before."
He smiled as he spoke and like a golden yolk,
his tooth lit up the floor.

All around it seemed, like some happy dream,
were coins of brightest gold.
They shone, shimmered, sparkled and glittered,
such a wonder to behold.

He saw my eyes, and my surprise,
to see where a moment ago,
was naught but stone, beneath his throne,
but now with gold did glow.

"Nothing makes sense, it is all pretense,
you scarce believe your eyes.
So what is true? What should you do?
No truth and so many lies."

He waved his hand and at this command,
a bell dropped from on high.
"I think you've heard, this dainty bird,
call you from the sky."

In the corner of my eye, in shadow I spied,
  a butterfly of green.
A voice in my head then softly said,
  "Discard what you have seen.

"Trust not your eyes, be not surprised,
  by what this liar might do.
Trust your nose and ears and do not fear,
  for I am here with you.

"I know him of old, he and his gold,
  he'll tempt you with false words.
If ever you knew, a love that's true,
  heed what you now have heard."

Somehow I knew these words were true,
  and then I smelled her scent.
The Lady in Green in that woodland scene;
  back, back my memory went.

"Come, take this gold, for if truth be told,
  with it I am so bored.
There is so much, it's very touch,
  too much for me to store.

"Take what you wish, for I ask only this,
  that you give to me your name."
He then stepped down onto the ground,
  "Come and stake your claim."

The voice in my head, warned me instead,
    that this was no simple matter.
This was his means, by which to glean,
    my thoughts through idle chatter.

He was the Liar, who from Hell's fire,
    was a master of illusion.
'Though the gold was real, I could well feel,
    his strategy was confusion.

In an amiable way, he proceeded to say,
    "Come. Come and take your fill.
There's plenty here, so do not fear,
    to take whatever you will.

"Take any and aught, for you have sought,
    this very Mountain, I know.
You left your home and came alone,
    so long . . . so long, long ago."

The green butterfly, did by and by,
    in shadow and in light,
fly here and there and soon came near,
    on me did then alight.

'Though behind me now, somewhere, somehow,
    I seemed to hear it speak.
My Lady's voice, my heart rejoiced -
    she whom I did seek.

I thought to turn, for the Lady's return,
    filled me with such delight.
I thought to say, beg her to stay,
    my heart was again light.

But 'though I thought, I saw her not,
    there was only he and I.
But still I heard her whispered words,
    her breathing and her sighs.

"Come, come," said he with a look of glee,
    his eyes and smile enticed me.
"This is your treasure. It is my pleasure.
    Take it quick and flee.

"Will you have more, than lies on this floor?
    Perhaps you wish some gems?"
He closed his eyes, let out a sigh,
    "Come, take your fill my friend."

My eyes opened wide, as there I spied,
    sparkling between the gold,
jewels great and small, 'neath the waterfall,
    so beautiful to behold.

XVII

So often I've heard, such foolish words,
    that I never could believe.
To sell one's soul, for a handful of gold,
    what fool could that conceive?
Yet the human heart, can be torn apart,
    when subject to temptation.
Men's prayers struck dumb, they all succumb,
    and earn the Devil's damnation.

Sapphires sea-blue and red rubies too,
    emeralds and diamonds bright.
They shimmered and shone, those precious stones,
    like stars in the darkest night.

I bent down to feel. They were all too real!
    'Though absent but moments ago.
I picked one up, on a golden cup,
    it's luster all aglow.

He laughed aloud, like a mighty crowd,
    the noise rang in my ears.
That mocking sound, echoed around,
    naught else could I hear.

But then I heard, my Lady's words,
    whispered soft but clear.
"Keep safe you name, 'though play his game,
    do not his magic fear."

"Why hesitate?" he then did state.
    "This is but part of the whole.
Come, take what you wish, a little of this,
    for was that not your goal?"

I saw him grin, as there I squirmed;
    he knew my will was weak.
For it was true you see, that the reality,
    temptation stole my speech.

His demeanor changed, he now seemed strange,
he seemed to lose his patience.
He floated to me, that he might see,
why I lacked obeisance.

"Why hesitate? Let us not debate,
the reason for your quest.
It is plain to me, quite plain to see.
Be no more distressed."

His peculiar eyes did hypnotize,
as he looked into my soul.
With a cat-like stare, he held me there,
amongst the jewels and gold.

I saw the fire, flames burning higher,
in those deep and gaping holes.
And I thought I heard, the anguished words,
of tortured, tormented souls.

From far away, they seemed to say,
that I should flee that place.
Run from the Mount and the golden fount,
and seek the Good Lord's Grace.

In life they fell, from grace to tell,
their stories and their deceit.
But those poor, dear men, far my ken,
for release they did me entreat.

I covered my ears, lest I should hear,
    their anguished pleas and more.
As their screams and shouts, echoed about,
    I fell senseless to the floor.

But as I fell, I heard her tell,
    my Lady's voice was clear.
"Fear not to sleep, for I shall keep,
    beside you far and near."

XVIII

Someone once said, that living or dead,
    the love of gold was a sin.
We should live our lives, free of vice,
    and so enter Heaven therein.
But on the Mountain trail, every man has failed,
    to live beyond a day.
For there it is said, the souls of the dead,
    are tried and tormented always.

In fearful dreams, I passed it seems,
    the remainder of that day.
When somewhere I heard, a wistful word,
    that urged me, escape, away!

My heart sank fast in that place of dark,
    and my eyes soon opened wide.
But everywhere, as I looked and stared,
    I thought that I had died!

In the night it seemed I escaped my dreams,
    and now they swallowed me whole.
I prayed and cried, for the light denied,
    that dreadful night had stole.

Then light in hand, traversed the land,
    my Lady of the glen,
came close to me, that I might see,
    the most beautiful of women.

"Be not afraid," to me she said,
    as her light shone ever bright.
"Have no fear, for I am near,
    to guide you through this night."

"How came you here?" I asked in fear,
    my voice, trembling and low.
I took her hand and up did stand,
    warming in her glow.

For the air was cold, like the taste of gold,
    an eerie silence lay around.
And echoing there, in the Mountain's air,
    reverberated every sound.

"Let not him claim your one true name,
    lest he seize your soul."
That Lady fair, in my despair,
    gave me more than gold.

"This man of sin, will seek to win,
    both you and your soul.
For torment awaits, through Hell's gates,
    if you succumb to his gold."

My mouth was dry, I heard her sigh,
    her scent was fresh and sweet.
In that dismal air, she seemed so fair,
    I fell down at her feet.

"Forgive I pray, my foolish ways,"
    I said deep from my heart.
"My spirit is weak, for I did seek,
    this Mountain from the start."

My tears rolled down and hit the ground,
    turning quick to steam.
She saw surprise, stream from my eyes;
    I thought I was in dream.

I recalled my home and my mother alone,
    and my father as he left.
I missed them so, so long ago,
    there I was truly blessed.

It rent my heart, full wide apart,
    I thought that I would die.
So much pain, I felt it again,
    and set once more to cry.

She touched my chin, so soft her skin,
    my heart was truly pained.
But I dried my tears to face my fears,
    and stood a man again.

She came to me and I could see,
    compassion in her face.
Her endearing smile, did me beguile,
    such beauty filled with grace.

"This Mountain place," she turned her face,
    "is not what you might think."
That Woodland Daughter took some water,
    and urged me then to drink.

That Mountain water, for me a pauper,
    glistened bright like gold.
Unlike the fires of Hell and that ringing bell,
    this whiskey was bitter cold.

But whiskey still—so I took my fill,
at first it pleased my tongue.
But slowly then, it changed again,
to the taste of farmyard dung!

I spat it out, on the ground about,
my stomach heaved and cried.
I felt so ill, near lost my will,
I thought that I would die.

But soon it passed, as quick I cast,
that disgusting, bitter brew.
Then she gave me wine, as an anodyne,
I stood again renewed.

"How can this be?" I asked of she.
"What is happening here?"
Her loving smile, calmed me awhile,
dispelling quite my fear.

She touched my head and whispering said,
"Most wealth is but illusion.
His purpose is, your soul to twist,
and cause you much confusion.

"His earnest task, is but to grasp,
that which is yours alone.
And through your name, he seeks to gain,
possession of your soul.

"When Hell's bell rings, paupers and Kings,
all tremble to hear that sound.
For then the souls who covet such gold,
know his demons are around.

"They seek those who, will drink their brew,
made in the pit of Hell.
But they never do think that to take that drink,
rings the Devil's bell.

"And when it rings, the demons sing;
they delight to hear that sound.
Then they take their prey, by night and day,
and bring them underground.

"Men's love of gold, gives them control,
over their hearts and will.
With promises false, to this Mountain vault,
they bring their bodies to kill.

"At the peal of the bell, the hordes of Hell,
ride swift over all the land.
With the Devil's gold, they tempt men's souls,
and forever they are damned."

I gave a gasp, before I asked,
"So this is Hell, is it not?
This Mountain here, is then I fear,
the place that I have sought."

Then I felt the fear again draw near,
    and the smell of burning flesh,
came over the air as I stood there,
    fear-filled, I do confess.

For my father dear, was somewhere here,
    ‘though thought of wealth now gone.
What should I do? I would construe,
    a plan as befits a son.

XIX

When the moon rises high in the midnight sky,
    they say the Devil rides fast.
Of his evil stare, we should all be aware,
    lest on us a spell he casts.
In the Mountain of Gold, burn countess souls,
    whenever Hell's bell does chime.
If you hear it there, beware! Beware!
    It will call us all sometime.

The Mountain cave, might be my grave,
    where my soul might ever burn.
In my Lady's care, standing there,
    I searched which way to turn.

That Mountain seemed like a fearful dream,
    I wished no more to stay.
Then I heard a sound, come from the ground,
    I wished I could fast away.

From out the ground, came a ghastly sound—
    the cries of screaming in pain.
He quick appeared, his face and beard;
    Satan rose from his domain.

In my Lady's stead, I saw instead,
    that butterfly of green.
But quick she went, behind me sent,
    she remained there quite unseen.

"Who are you?" he asked. "Speak true.
    If you lie be sure, I'll know.
"Though you have such gold, I have my soul,
    to Hell I shall not go.

"My name is mine and never thine,
    it is no concern of yours.
If you give me thine, I may give mine—
    Of this you can be sure."

My words were bold, yet his tooth of gold,
    shone bright through his smile.
'Though I did speak, my legs were weak,
    as he grinned all the while.

"Well! Well spoken!" he said without emotion,
    as he looked around the Mount.
"Your courage and bravery are plain to see,
    but look! See what I have found!"

He laughed aloud, as a veritable crowd,
    of demons filled that cave.
They spat and hissed, from a stinking mist,
    as to me they then clave.

My mouth was dry, I thought to cry,
    and plead for my deliverance.
But my voice had gone, I thought me done,
    amidst their hideous dissonance.

Some grinned and smiled, some laughed awhile;
    I thought to kneel and pray.
I knew right then, that the souls of men,
    were their preferred prey.

But they had not seen, my Butterfly green,
    my Lady whispered again.
"Stand your ground and make no sound,
    be a man amongst men."

I stood stock still, steeling my will,
    to do as I was told.
'Though filled with fear, as they drew near,
    deep in that Mount of Gold.

My face was a mask, for to do my task,
    I must learn to seal my lips.
My Lady Green, by them unseen,
    with courage did me equip.

"Speak now!" said he. "Tell to me,
    the name by which you are known.
If you withhold, this treasure of gold,
    will all to soon be gone."

I heard her say in her gentle way,
    words to guide in that place.
Keep safe my name, lest he should claim,
    my soul to my disgrace.

"I came here not, as you seem to have thought,
    for gold or any other treasure.
For this I'll say, if you care to stay,
    the price of my single pleasure."

The demons stopped, their faces dropped,
    to hear me speak without fear.
Then the Devil smiled, his tooth shone wild.
    The smiled then turned to a leer.

"And what can you, tell me that's new?
    That I've not heard before?
Through all my days, mere curses or praise,
    no souls have been restored.

"For eventually, they all come to me,
    for men are weak of will.
They search for gold, risking their souls,
    and all men search it still.

"So, come now, start! I know your heart,
    and what you most desire.
Say what you must, for in this you can trust,
    you may yet fuel Hell's fires."

His tooth of gold shone as he extolled,
    the power of his dark art.
The misery that awaited me,
    when I would this life depart.

The tales he told, froze my bones,
    and visions passed before my eyes,
More dreadful to me that any might believe,
    or conceived by the wicked or wise.

There passed an age, 'ere I assuaged,
    the nightmare of those sights.
As they slowly passed, my gaze was cast,
    upon a mysterious device.

Shining and bold, I saw his bell of gold,
 floating high in the air.
Above that host, of demons and ghosts,
 for its chime I did prepare.

I knew that bell, for it came from Hell;
 it rang when a soul was lost.
As that host of ghouls, began to drool;
 my head and chest I crossed.

I saw that man, with a gong in hand,
 raise high the bell to strike,
Hell's bell of gold, above that fold,
 with all his evil might.

XX

There once was a man from a far distant land,
  who told me the strangest tale.
He spoke of the sky, that he saw on high,
  as it rose above a Mountain trail.
He said that the Devil, was on the level,
  and his horde was quite benign.
And a Mountain of Gold, was home to the souls,
  of the wise and the kind.

Up shot my hand and before it could land,
    the Devil stopped and said,
"Be quick to speak, else I shall keep,
    your soul when you are dead!"

My Lady Green, hidden from that scene,
    guided my every word.
Her pure, clear voice, rose above the noise,
    of those demons undeterred.

"If you would know, the high and low,
    of all there is on earth.
What will you give that I might live,
    that I might be of worth?

"For I have here, such cunning clear,
    my possession is mighty indeed.
It's worth is more, than all your store;
    your gold it does exceed."

"Aha!" said he, with a chuckle of glee,
    "I like the cut of your jib.
But it's futile you see, to contest with me,
    so I'd advise you, no more glib.

"Well . . . well I suppose, you now will propose,
    some means by which you might flee?
But let me tell you, that this much is true,
    you'll never now be free."

I felt his stare, as he held me there,
    fearful right down to my bones.
His steely stare, exposed me bare,
    naked, like a shore-washed stone.

But 'though I feared, as he drew near,
    I kept safe and secure.
With my Lady's aid, I need not be afraid,
    of that I could be sure.

Yet still I did try, some courage to ply,
    that he might not discover.
But that golden bell, an evil death-knell,
    above me still did hover.

"Speak, speak," said he, "for as you can see,
    I am a most reasonable man.
But I haven't all day, so let's hear you say,
    and I'll do whatever I can."

My mind was a gale, for I had no tale,
    that I might to him tell.
I searched for words, when horror! I heard,
    the ringing of the bell!

XXI

I once heard tell, of a fearsome bell,
    that sounds on the Mountain trail.
That sound so clear, strikes men with fear,
    like the hammering of a nail.
That bell of gold calls to men's souls,
    and 'though they fear it's ring,
their unbridled greed, damnation feeds,
    and drives insatiable sin.

That awful sound did me surround,
    I covered my ears in pain.
Like an age and more, I lay on that floor,
    'til I could rise again.

But he laughed to see, my infirmity,
    and the anguish on my face.
'Though my legs were weak, I still did seek,
    escape from that Mountain place.

"What say you now? Come, speak somehow,
    that I might spare your life.
Come tell me why, you should not die,
    and spare you from Hell's strife."

I heard her voice amidst that noise,
    of Hell's hideous demons.
For my flesh they craved, my soul enslave,
    that horde of Hell's legions.

I looked around as that Hellish sound,
    calmed and then was gone.
"What must I do, to satisfy you,
    that the luster of gold is worn?"

I sounded bold, when I spoke of gold,
    I was a man again it seemed.
And as I spoke, his interest awoke;
    his tooth glistened and gleamed.

I saw through his smile and attempt to beguile,
    and thus to win my soul.
He waved his hand and all the sand,
    in that Mountain shone like gold.

He waved again and there appeared a man,
    whom I recognised so well.
His form and face, by the Lord's Good Grace,
    was trapped by the Devil's spell.

XXII

When the full moon glistens, if you care to listen,
    you might hear the North wind tell,
of the Mountain trail, where men turn pale,
    when they hear Beelzebub's bell.
That Hellish alarm, does mortal harm,
    as it's chime rings all around.
And if you chance, to see the Devil dance,
    you'll forever regret that sound.

Through a misty gaze, as in a drunken haze,
 I saw my father dear,
contort and twist, as the demons hissed,
 and then I saw him clear.

He said not a word, remaining unheard,
 as I crossed the golden sand.
As I reached out, I thought to shout,
 when I felt the Devil's hand.

"Come, come my friend, rules you may bend,
 but they cannot here be broken.
Speak if you must, but I insist, I trust,
 obey that which I have spoken.

"His soul is mine, as will be thine,
 you must accept this fact.
No use to try, or ask me why,
 his soul is forever trapped.

"But I'll tell to you, if you tell me true,
 I'll wager you for your soul.
If you should desire, to avoid Hell's fire,
 you still may have my gold.

"Will you gold take and your father forsake,
 perchance wager for his soul?
Ask me aught, for his soul I have bought,
 let not my offer grow cold.

"I'll prove my skill, if you would kill,
all thought of leaving here.
Stay with me and you shall see,
the wonders of my sphere.

"And you shall live for I shall give
you knowledge, wealth and power.
What say you now? Will you allow,
or will you play the coward?"

Far in my mind, I sought to find,
some way to answer him.
Some words to say, my fear to slay,
and my freedom there to win.

My tongue stuck fast, until at last,
my Lady guided me.
My courage returned, his offer spurned,
my words echoed eerily.

"I'll not be turned, in Hell to burn,
'though I came for treasure indeed.
Although you show, your treasures aglow,
for release I shall not plead.

"For I have more, than all your stores,
that you or Hell could hold.
So I challenge you, to a bitter duel,
that you might keep your gold."

His smile grew bold, amidst his gleaming gold,
his horde of demons laughed.
He thought a while and again he smiled,
as of me then he asked.

"I've heard the speech, that you've unleashed;
your words are indeed bold.
So do you propose, do you suppose,
you can win *his* soul?

"For countless have tried and all have died,
and here forever they remain.
And yet you say, to me convey,
a challenge in my domain?

"You have heart perhaps, to so attack,
you have some measure of a man.
You stand so proud, your words speak loud,
but no weapon in your hand.

"Perchance this toy, that fools employ,
you think will save you today.
But dispel this myth," he said with a hiss,
as with my gun he played.

I looked around; found naught but ground,
I saw there by my side.
My pistol gone, like the vanishing dawn,
and no-where there to hide.

He laughed once more, as he'd done before;
    he reveled in my confusion.
His demons growled, around they prowled,
    I prayed it was illusion.

Once more I feigned, courage regained,
    that I had no fear of him.
Her voice so clear, whispered in my ear,
    and soon his smile dimmed.

"I have travelled far, beneath sun and stars,
    to find the Mountain of Gold.
I journeyed and came, to the Mountain acclaimed,
    to confirm what I'd been told.

"It's true I found, as is here around,
    the Mountain is filled with gold.
But there's more here, than gold I fear—
    dead men and their souls.

"But what I wish, is simply this—
    I wish to know *your* name.
Give me but that before I pass,
    and I shall give you the same.

"Not much to ask—a trifling task,
    that is what we civilized do.
A fair exchange, that we might arrange,
    a dialogue that's true.

"What say you? Come, tell me true,
 give me now your name.
Let us converse and together traverse,
 this playful little game."

As he perused, he saw my ruse,
 I saw gold glint again.
Only untruths, from his golden tooth,
 on this I might depend.

It came to this, our battle of wits,
 in which we now engaged.
The game was afoot, around I looked;
 victory alone could assuage.

But he was no fool, amidst his gold and jewels,
 he looked long and hard.
He considered awhile and then he smiled,
 he saw through my façade.

XXIII

I've heard it said, that the souls of the dead,
    toil in the Mountain of Gold.
In the fires of Hell, I've heard men tell,
    by the Devil's legions controlled.
All rest denied, devoid of pride,
    they do the Devil's will.
To mine his gold, those piteous souls,
    ever toil there still.

"No, no my friend, do not offend,
who has power over your soul.
Do not tempt me, if you would be free.
Come, fill your pockets with gold.

"But let us suppose, that of all those,
you have a ready wit.
Would you dare challenge, my mighty talent?
To me you will submit.

"But this trifling matter, this idle chatter,
is not worthy of such as you.
What's in a name, a mere child's game?
Perhaps I'll not speak true."

I heard his speech, as his demons unleashed,
vile hisses and curses loud.
But I stood there still and steeled my will,
to battle that Hellish crowd.

He raised his hand and at his command,
that Horde fell once more quiet.
With menacing grins, those demons of sin,
ceased their evil riot.

"Come tell to me," then said he,
"Why you wish to know my name.
Tell me but this and I'll dismiss,
these creatures whence they came."

"As I said before," my speech restored,
  "some semblance of our art.
For we both are, like a door ajar,
  welcoming 'ere we part.

"You must know, 'ere I bestow,
  my title to you make known.
That you must say, before the end of day,
  the name that is your own.

"As I have asked, that you do this task,
  I'll half or letter my name.
But if I begin, I'm sure to win,
  the object of this game.

"So let's start now and then somehow,
  we'll settle this matter at last.
I'll take your gold and keep my soul,
  and put you in the past."

His tooth shone bright, in the golden light,
  as he smiled and looked at me.
He thought some more as he crossed the floor,
  then took my hand with glee.

XXIV

The Devil's gold, so I've been told,
    is rarely kept by men.
And those who search, on his trident perch,
    and are never seen again.
For if it they seek, on them is wreaked,
    the Devil's malignant charm.
And in a Mountain tall, their souls soon fall,
    into Hell's eternal storm.

"Then come with me and you shall see,"
 he said as he took my hand.
As up we rose, how could I suppose,
 where I would eventually land?

I blinked and sighed, as I saw the sky,
 the clouds and bright firmament.
How through we passed that Mountain vast,
 there is no determinant.

But nonetheless, I must confess,
 as up we rose on high,
the land around with such beauty endowed,
 spread out to meet the sky.

Still higher we rose, that I supposed,
 I might never again return.
Then my heart feared, as the moon drew near,
 I prayed my flight adjourn.

But the Devil laughed more, as on we soared;
 the valley below grew dim.
The sun fell low, beneath the earth below,
 I felt the cold within.

Higher and high, beyond the sky,
 the valley below disappeared.
And through the clouds, like silver shrouds,
 my butterfly reappeared.

Her song-like voice, my heart rejoiced,
to hear her comforting words.
Reassuring me, I looked to see,
and felt no more disturbed.

"All that you see, belongs to me,
for the world is my footstool.
If you consider this, and so reminisce,
it is a mighty jewel.

"I shall grant it you, if you remain true,
and sign my book of contract.
Then Master you'll be and soon you'll see,
such riches to be tapped."

I met his gaze, in the sun's dying rays,
as he smiled his tooth shone bright.
I felt the cold, like the kiss of gold.
Beyond him was darkest night.

"A generous gift, dare I admit,"
I said as I looked down.
"But the world is small, when you consider all,
that in the universe abounds.

"My blood is mine, a gift Devine,
given to me by another.
I'll not let it flow, to stain the earth below,
disrespecting my father and mother.

"So if you would know, let's go below,
    and return to the world of men.
This tiresome flight, at such great height,
    has made me hungry again."

In a flash we returned, where Hell's fires burned,
    I felt his anger rise.
In the Mountain again, in the world of men,
    I looked into his eyes.

Cat-like spheres, I felt my fear,
    as I caught a glimpse of Hell.
The tortured souls, where eternity unrolled,
    and ever the ringing of the bell.

But I gathered strength and then at length,
    he turned away and said,
"Avarice is good but I see your mood,
    is turned to wisdom instead.

"Do you think it wise, that such a prize,
    is left unclaimed by you?
Come, come my friend, let's put to an end,
    and say that which is true."

But in my ear, I firm could hear,
    the voice of clearest wisdom.
"Mephistopheles," (he looked with glee)
    I thought my task was done.

XXV

A man once said, that in his head,
he heard the Devil speak.
He tormented him, his soul to win,
beneath that Mountain peak.
The promise of gold, in that Mount of souls,
was more than he could bear.
In that Mountain of Gold, he lost his soul,
to his eternal despair.

We returned to ground, as I felt around,
    the earth beneath my feet.
The Mountain tall, made me feel small,
    'though the country air smelled sweet.

Above my head, the sky turned red,
    as the sun fell far away.
My belly sighed, for food I cried,
    as I watched the dying day.

With a Devilish grin, that man of sin,
    he saw my need and smiled.
Into the Mount, to the golden fount,
    he led me like a child.

"I see . . . I think, you need a drink,
    and hunger too I see."
His measured words, were what I heard,
    as still he grinned at me.

He stooped to ground and there he found,
    a smooth stone in his palm.
He held it out, I had no doubt,
    a stone lay in his hand.

"It's true," I said, as he raised his head,
    "my hunger is great indeed."
"Come, eat you fill," he told me still.
    "Sit, at my table and feed."

I bare believed, I bare did breath,
as a table suddenly appeared.
Laden with fare, delicious and rare,
and he drew me near.

"But not for this," as I dismissed,
the food before my eyes.
Then a smell arose, joy to my nose,
knowledge to the wise.

Before me lay, (dare it I say),
in his outstretched hand,
no stone, instead—a wafer of bread,
in the palm of the damned.

"Come, come good Sir," his words I heard,
as he ate that wafer of bread.
As on I looked, his grin I brooked,
there lay another instead.

Each one he ate, like some magical plate,
there came another in it's place.
It was magic indeed, that he did cede,
each wafer in that place.

"Come, come feast! Let your hunger cease,
Come! Let us dine and drink.
This delicious wine and bread so fine,
you'll enjoy it . . . I do think."

My Lady's words, then I heard,
so clearly in my head,
that I turned to him, his supercilious grin,
and boldly, then I said.

"I hunger, yes but food unblessed,
I cannot deign to eat.
Such a disgrace, I cannot face,
so alone you must feast."

His smile disappeared and a look of fear,
glanced across his leering face.
His shining grin and thoughts of sin,
lost at the mention of Grace.

His hand he waved, interrupting Grace,
and the banquet too was gone.
Unlike his smile, now filled with guile,
he approached me then with scorn.

XXVI

A man's own dreams, to me it seems,
    are but desires of his heart.
On that Mountain trail, where demons wail,
    bodies and souls will part.
When I consider, the sweet and the bitter,
    and all my life has been,
I shake and shudder in utter wonder,
    at all that I have seen.

Increasing rage showed on his face,
as he flew across the ground.
My heart beat fast, but oh! Alas!
I dare not return his frown.

My feet stuck firm, 'though I tried to turn,
I was paralyzed with fear.
His face transformed, his head horned,
a loud thudding in my ear.

His body burned, as to me he returned,
with a tail of fiery red.
His feet were hooves and as he moved,
I heard her in my head.

"This is your hour, he has no power,
if you can still hold fast.
Do not bow down, upon the ground,
else this day be your last."

I was so relieved, I all but believed,
I was lost in utter Hell.
In the Mountain's heart, by the Devil's art,
I feared to hear that bell.

For if it rang, the Devil's harangue,
would be my eternal reward.
He sought my soul, to burn like coal,
to amuse his Hellish horde.

His snake-like tongue, like fire burned;
    I felt the heat from his face.
He looked at me, (my fear plain to see);
    he thought me to debase.

I saw in his eyes, contempt arise,
    as he considered what to do.
A hissing sound, seemed all around,
    as he looked me through and through.

At his command was a trident in hand,
    as he screamed a deafening curse.
He struck my head and contemptuously said,
    he wished he could do worse.

All in a moment, my veritable opponent,
    was gone and quite away.
As my sight faded, my senses vacated,
    and I dreamed of happier days.

XXVII

In a tavern of old, a tale was told,
    by a traveler on the Mountain trail.
Plain to see was the look of glee,
    when avarice prevailed.
For the pursuit of wealth at expense of health,
    is but a foolish man's quest.
If he covets only gold, he'll lose his soul,
    and never, ever find rest.

Beneath a darkened sky I opened my eyes;
    the air felt sharp and cold.
I thought I was dead, save for my head,
    wherein a mighty bell tolled.

Then whispering I heard inside my head—
    my Lady was with me there.
'Though the air was dark, by the stars' sparks,
    I saw her face glow fair.

But my head ached, 'though Mountain escaped,
    I was dazed and so confused.
Perhaps a dream, the Devil's scream,
    the bell and demons I mused.

"Quick, rise and run, before the sun,
    is risen in the sky."
Her lilting voice; her advice employed,
    I rose, her counsel to comply.

A horse stood near, a trusty steer,
    I mounted quick and flew.
But the night was black, on that Mountain track,
    and soon my fear renewed.

The bell loud tolled as I felt the cold,
    creep through to my bones.
The wind blew round with a howling sound,
    ahead I heard a groan.

XXVIII

In a song I heard, that the Devil's word,
is false and filled with guile.
That eternal liar, in Hell's great fire,
will win you with his smile.
So the avaricious, like young Narcissus,
will be quick to lose their souls.
For that wily fiend, will kill their dreams,
if they think to win his gold.

My horse reared, as ahead appeared,
    a light from beneath a door.
A wooden hut, it's door fast shut,
    my safety might be restored.

Towards it I rode, for there I proposed,
    beg shelter from the wind's harm.
The door I pushed, inside I rushed,
    sheltered from the storm.

An empty space, before me graced,
    a haven from the storm.
Before me there, I do declare,
    a fire burned bright and warm.

And none but I, as the storm passed by,
    stood in that place of light.
And there I passed, the night at last,
    my dreams were glowing bright.

The following morn, I saw the dawn,
    the fire had all burned out.
The storm had gone, its havoc done,
    I was safe, I had no doubt.

The sun rose high, in a bright, blue sky,
    devoid of a single cloud.
As I breathed the air, without a care,
    I saw that Mountain proud!

My heart beat fast, I coughed, I gasped,
    how could this be? I thought.
Fast beat my heart at the Devil's art;
    my weapon and horse I sought.

I heard a sound, as I looked around,
    behind a twig then snapped.
I held my breath, as I thought of death,
    quite certain I was trapped.

"Oh my! Oh me!" I heard from the trees,
    "Who on earth is this?"
A gentle speech, the silence breached,
    as I gathered there my wits.

XXIX

In my moments alone, safe in my home,
	I think on all that's been.
When I eat my bread, lay down my head,
	I crave forgiveness in dreams.
For yes, I was tempted, morally emptied,
	when in that Mountain of Gold.
But it was no surprise that in his eyes,
	the Devil had no soul.

Before me stood, at the edge of the wood,
    fresh game on her shoulder.
A dark-haired girl, with eyes like pearls,
    her foot upon a boulder.

"I see you've found, my humble compound,
    it saved you from the storm.
Lucky for me," continued she,
    "it did me no harm.

"It came up so fast," she smiled, she laughed,
    "it caught me quite by surprise.
So I stayed in the woods, as long as I could."
    The sun glistened in her eyes.

"I guess you're starved," (she looked at me hard).
    "Looks like you've hardly eaten.
Come on, let's eat, we'll have a feast;
    the storm's been well beaten."

So in I entered, to hunger surrendered,
    into that tiny, wooden cabin.
We cooked the game on the fire's flame;
    better than I could imagine.

So my hunger satiated, we both then waited,
    we talked and passed the time.
Telling tales of old, the Mountain of Gold,
    the Devil and the Divine.

She asked me to stay, with her that day.
  I agreed and stayed that night.
In the morning we rose when she proposed,
  we scaled the Mountain's height.

Ignorance I feigned, of the Mountain acclaimed;
  she laughed in disbelief.
"Why lie to me?" she asked with glee,
  "Trust me—I am no thief."

I held my ruse, I quite refused,
  to tell her what I knew.
But she saw through me and said with glee.
  "You've drunk the Devil's brew."

My mouth opened wide, as I desperately tried,
  to maintain my foolish deceit.
But it was quite futile, I could not beguile,
  this girl who seemed so sweet.

I resorted to silence, my tacit defiance,
  was all I could think of then.
But I knew she knew, I was untrue.
  I was the worst of men.

She giggled and laughed, until at last,
  she confessed she knew of gold.
But the hidden Mount, could not be found,
  save by the boldest of bold.

I told her then, only foolish men,
    took note of such a story.
A Mountain of Gold! I sneered and cajoled.
    She was the Devil's quarry.

So she told me more, of mud and gore,
    her life she'd spent in searching.
Ten years she'd spent, as malcontent;
    reading, hunting and learning.

She had heard the tale, of the Mountain trail,
    when but an innocent girl.
And to find the gold, as she'd been told,
    she'd searched the entire world.

XXX

If you ever do think, Devil's whiskey to drink,
    I counsel severe restraint.
The Devil's brew, I'll tell you true,
    would turn the saintliest saint.
The Mountain trail is no idle tale,
    for I'm the only one,
who took that path, of which you ask,
    and only I have returned.

For a day we talked, in the woods we walked;
    she ever talked of gold.
My ignorance maintained, no knowledge I claimed,
    through the day I quietly lolled.

The tale I told, was not of gold,
    but the story of my home.
I had little to say save I'd left one day,
    and the country I had roamed.

Adventures completed, my quest secreted;
    I thought she believed my tale.
She asked me to stay, for one more day,
    'ere I took my homeward trail.

So that night we ate, ending our debate,
    on the merits of pursuing wealth.
But her view held firm—she would not turn.
    A great blow would soon be dealt.

That night I crept into bed and slept,
    I sensed the girl was awake.
In my ruse to keep, I feigned deep sleep,
    and made such a dreadful mistake.

This nocturnal explorer, searched for water,
    but finding none she left.
In the dead of night, she left my sight,
    in dreams I then soundly slept.

XXXI

I never could tell, if the sound of that bell,
    was real or in my head.
Yet still I fear its sound to hear,
    when nightmares reach my bed.
In the Mountain of Gold, where those poor souls,
    bear unspeakable torture,
The Devil holds court, on those he fought,
    while his demons obey his orders.

As the sun rose high, into the blue sky,
    I woke to hear bird song.
The air smelled sweet and from the east,
    a breeze blew soft and long.

I walked to the river and in it's mirror,
    I saw my haggard face.
My hair awry, 'neath that azure sky,
    I thought I was a disgrace.

So I washed in the water, as I thought of her,
    the girl who had left that night.
Where had she gone? What had she done?
    Departing with no torch or light?

And here in the morning, I felt a warning,
    somewhere in my heart.
But I left well alone, such doubts I bemoaned,
    thinking I would soon depart.

I roused with a start, as a beat missed my heart,
    and a shot went over my head!
The water turned cold, right though to my soul;
    another made it run red.

'Though the water was cold, like the taste of gold,
    my leg burned sulphur and fire.
A bullet was lodged, some damage it caused,
    as was her deliberate desire.

On the bank she stood, behind her the wood,
with a rifle in her hands.
From the barrel came smoke, as she then spoke,
demanding I climb on land.

I pressed my leg, where the river ran red,
to halt the flow of blood.
The pain was intense, I near lost my sense,
as I stood there in the flood.

As naked as a babe, no thought of escape,
and injured through to my bone,
I begged her no more, as I made to the shore,
and rested on a stone.

She ordered me up, as was my luck.
I asked her what she desired.
She laughed out loud, as I sat there cowed,
and asked for the warmth of a fire.

I took my clothes and made the most,
of somehow binding my wound.
In the cabin I lay, like a naked babe,
with pain I was consumed.

I dressed myself, such pain I felt,
and sat upon the bed.
As I looked at her, strange thoughts stirred,
as a bell rang in my head.

XXXII

When the clouds turn dark and the only sparks,
    are stars lighting the sky,
on the Mountain trail, when the night prevails,
    beware the bats flying by.
Those agents of sin, your soul will win,
    if they catch you unawares.
If the Devil rides, be sure to hide,
    and be certain to say your prayers.

"Where'd you find this gold?" as she rolled,
    a shiny coin to me.
I picked it up and quite dumbstruck,
    she gave me the third degree.

Embossed with a bell and as I could tell,
    the coin was pure, solid gold.
On the other side, two horns I spied,
    and then my blood ran cold.

For the Devil's face, that coin graced,
    I recognized it immediately.
And in her hand as she there did stand,
    two coins more held she.

"Your saddle-bag's packed!" at me she snapped,
    as she pointed the rifle at me.
"Tell me now, or by God, somehow,
    I'll never let you leave.

"There's more I know, of this golden glow,
    at the end of the Mountain trail.
I've been searchin' these years and I ain't afeared,
    of the all them foolish tales.

"So if you agree, then you and me,
    we both can be rich quick.
But if you prefer, trouble to stir,
    I'll send you to Auld Nick."

I shrugged again and tried to feign,
    no answer to her question.
I had no idea, 'though quite afeard,
    I gave her my full attention.

It was truly so, that I did not know,
    how gold had just appeared.
My saddle bag, was all I had,
    but still she persevered.

"I want to know and we will go,
    to that there Mount of Gold.
I won't kill you, if you tell me true,
    and you can keep your soul.

"So tell me here, whisper in my ear,
    where you found this gold.
Then I'll tend to you, we'll drink a brew,
    and shelter from the cold.

"And when you're well, if you true tell,
    we'll both head for the trail.
And soon we'll find, the richest gold mine,
    when the Mountain we assail."

But I pleaded with her, I could not stir,
    any pot of Satan's trouble.
There was nothing I knew (this was true),
    for it sure had me puzzled.

The rifle's butt, hit my head and hurt,
    I screamed in utter pain.
"Don't test me, or you'll never be free,
    and I'll shoot you once again."

I knew she was mean, from what I had seen,
    I feared she might shoot me dead.
But far, far away, in a distant haze,
    a bell rang in my head.

XXXIII

If you ever think you might turn to drink,
    I counsel you think twice.
For the Devil's brew, will all subdue,
    and take your soul in a thrice.
The river of gold, like all mens' souls,
    flows forever and a day.
On the Mountain trail, the demons wail,
    and soulless bodies decay.

I fell to the ground, as my head spun round,
    and still that bell rang loud.
In the distance I heard, filthy, foul words,
    and saw the demon crowd.

When at last I awoke, I heard the stroke,
    of someone ringing that bell.
My hands were bound, as I lay on the ground.
    But where? I could not tell.

There in the dark, not a single spark,
    I saw to provide any light.
The air was still, I thought I'd been killed,
    and doomed to eternal night.

I called loud out, I did scream and shout,
    my voice echoed all around.
So I stood on my feet, in the darkness complete;
    I was not dead in the ground.

And again I found, when I heard that sound—
    the ringing of that dread bell.
But not in my head, for I was not dead;
    then I thought I was in Hell.

For I felt some heat, about me beat,
    and the smell of burning flesh.
Then I feared once more as I did before,
    adding to my distress.

Then a single star, I saw from afar,
    and another and yet one more.
And all too soon, like a fiery moon,
    I saw the demon horde.

XXXIV

On the Mountain trail, are many tales,
    of men who have gone astray.
In their quest for gold, they lost their souls,
    forever and a day.
But the wise it's said, unlike the dead,
    know well the secret of life.
They discard wealth in favor of health,
    caring for their children and wives.

My eyes opened wide, for I was inside,
that Mountain once again!
After all I'd done, the distance I'd run,
I must myself defend.

The horde drew near, fast rose my fear;
they hissed and spat and cursed.
Such vile words which ever I'd heard,
grew loud as the ground they traversed.

A golden light shone, the horde upon,
as the Devil walked before that throng.
He raised his hand and at his command,
they silenced their wicked song.

I saw the flash, of the smile he cast,
as he stood before me and stared.
His tooth of gold, shone bright but cold—
I knew he had me snared.

For behind him trod, in that Hellish abode,
the girl who shot me with her gun.
He took her hand and with her did stand—
united, both as one.

"So you have returned, my Prodigal Son!
Somehow I knew you would."
His words rang clear that I might hear;
received and understood.

"You see my friend, you are condemned,
    by one who sees the right.
This valiant maid, was by me paid,
    to demonstrate my might.

"Her womanly wiles and charming smiles,
    could not entice you here.
So she used brute force and so of course,
    brought you into my sphere.

"There are some I've found and others crowned,
    but she is quite unique.
Her love of gold means she has no soul;
    such havoc she has wreaked!

"You see by her smile, that her feminine guile,
    has been used to great effect.
She brought you back, when sense you lacked,
    and my offer you did reject.

"So let's end mystery and you and she,
    may have your last conversation.
Come, come my friend, this is the end,
    of your all too brief association."

I knew it then, that of all men,
    I had been such a fool!
I would now soon die and never know why,
    at the hands of this ghoul.

"Ask any and aught and she'll retort,
with truth I'll warrant you this.
She'll not disobey, nor dare she stray.
For you, this is my gift."

I considered awhile, as on she smiled,
such a grin of self-satisfaction.
My blood ran cold, amidst the gold—
this maid had no compassion.

I knew I would die, no use to cry,
my reward was certain death.
Strangely reconciled, I thought a while,
before I drew my last breath.

Fear left me then and a man again,
I looked her in the eye.
She had no heart, what use to start,
to ask her reasons why?

So up I spoke, my right invoked,
and asked her there her name.
Then a hateful stare she threw me there,
"Suba," she exclaimed.

XXXV

On the Mountain trail, when the moon shines pale,
    the Devil rides out with his horde.
He wins men's soul, with his cache of gold,
    and grants them Hell's reward.
The souls of the dead, it's often been said,
    are of his greatest concern.
To the Lord of Hell, when he rings his bell,
    for in Hell they'll forever burn.

"Suba Nahahas," she said. "Now pass,
from this life to the next.
And so I shall claim, reward for your shame,
for time I am sore pressed.

"So now my Lord, I'll take my reward,
and leave his soul to your taste.
If you give me my gold, exchanged for his soul,
I shall leave you now in haste."

"Quite, quite," said he, with a look of glee,
as he leered in my direction.
His hands up-raised as 'though in praise,
my time for apperception.

"A hundred times your weight, I told you straight,
I'll give you for his soul.
So take it now and quite disavow,
how you earned this gold."

Then from on high, there came a sigh,
that soon became a rumble.
Down it rolled, a shower of gold,
in a loud and mighty tumble.

Suba cried aloud, as her golden shroud,
fell heavily all around.
Her body crushed, to golden dust,
laid silent in the ground.

XXXVI

To keep one's soul, make not your goal,
    riches on this earth.
So I've been told, for the taste of gold,
    is bitter and without worth.
In the Devil's mount, I scarce could count,
    the number of coins of gold.
Like the stars at night, they shone out bright—
    each one a dead man's soul.

His laugh rang round, a hideous sound,
    that echoed in my head.
When he'd had his fill, the air was still;
    I thought me now sure dead.

But he thought a while and drew a smile,
    and beckoned me come near.
He had something to say, so I made my way,
    his words then to hear.

"Can't you see," he said thoughtfully,
    "the humor of it all?
She took her gold, I took her soul.
    Don't look so appalled!

"She asked for gold, with no thought for her soul—
    am I to be blamed for that?
Avarice is rife, in most men's wives—
    accept this simple fact.

"There's no denying, that she's now lying,
    dead beneath her treasure.
Her soul is mine, in this my shrine—
    part of my eternal pleasure.

"Do not be concerned, you'll not be burned,
    in this or any other way.
You're far too precious, so come now let us . . .
    Sit, eat . . . stay.

"But do not despair, I do declare,
    your face is quite a sight!
Come let us dine on food so fine,
    we'll quite forget this night.

"Be not disturbed for my guests I'll curb,
    and dismiss them here and now.
And we shall discuss, our contract adjust,
    working together somehow.

"Take time to think, over a drink,
    and together we'll rule this world.
You see I have the power, you to empower—
    make ruler of this cosmic pearl.

"What say you now? Your field you'll plough,
    in this sorry world of men.
Their will is weak, for gold they seek.
    Salvation is beyond their ken.

"Their words are bold, as they search for gold.
    They store riches on this earth.
But all will die and so, by and by,
    they all will have no worth."

He nodded his head, as these words he said,
    and the demons all disappeared.
Like a lightening flash, gone and past,
    his smile—a sweet veneer.

"Aha, I see, I see . . . you still doubt me,
    and who can say you're wrong?
I know your mind, you think you'll find,
    with me you don't belong.

"But think on this as your mother's dear kiss,
    as dust beneath my feet.
Life everlasting, is yours for the asking;
    my victory is His defeat."

His statement made, I was sore afraid.
    Who was the "His" he referred?
But those lingering doubts, were plucked full out,
    in that Hell of souls interred.

Like the glorious sun, there was but One,
    who is worthy of such accolade.
In silent prayer, I beseeched Him there,
    to keep me safe I prayed.

"Come, tell to me," once more said he,
    "what troubles your restless heart?
Take comfort here and do not fear,
    to share with me your art.

"Your skill I know and of all below,
    you shall help me rule.
This world is mine and can be thine,
    if you will with me school.

"Give me your allegiance and your obeisance,
    and I promise all you desire.
Together we shall rule as masters of my ghouls—
    there is nothing we cannot acquire."

I looked at him, and as he sat and grinned,
    a mighty table appeared.
And there fast ensued, a feast of food,
    as my host laughed and leered.

"Come eat with me and you shall see,
    with clarity and with guile.
Live forever—die you shall never,
    beside me all the while.

"Come, sup and drink, say what you think,
    tell me of your thoughts.
Drop your head and you'll never be dead,
    and I'll deny you naught."

His servant be? Serve only he?
    Had I misheard his words?
I searched my soul, as men search for gold.
    Dare I believe what I heard?

XXXVII

Whenever I think, of the Devil's drink,
    when in the Mountain of Gold,
I shudder to recall, the memory of it all,
    that my soul I almost sold.
The sight of gold now leaves me cold;
    it has no allure for me.
And if you permit, I shall submit,
    to set men's souls free.

In that Mountain tomb, if I succumbed,
I would be forever prosperous.
But all I wished was my father exist.
The offer was preposterous!

I had far rather, give up my father,
than consent to be his slave.
I must away, before another day,
spent in that Mountain grave.

So I asked him stay, his proposal that day,
allow me yet some time.
We both should eat of that royal feast,
and drink the blood-red wine.

He cast a glance and I thought perchance,
he'd strike me down full dead.
But instead he poured, the wine like gore,
and smiling still, he said.

"You wish to ponder how you might squander,
your wealth and new found power?
No need to hurry, nor need to worry,
for this is your greatest hour."

So I ate the food, as best I could,
I drank his delicious wine.
But all the while, he sat and smiled,
I could not read his mind.

As we sat and ate, on golden plates,
    and drank from golden vessels,
he waved his hand and at this command,
    appeared a host of devils.

"Let's have a song and sing along,
    if you happen to know the tune."
He invited me, smiling gleefully,
    "We'll lift your spirits soon."

That demon group was a musical troupe;
    they began an infernal din.
What passed for song, was long and drawn,
    that hideous band of sin.

I prayed for release, that noise might cease,
    yet still the demons played.
I stilled my hand, amongst that band,
    resorting to silent prayer.

But why should He, pay heed to me?
    I never had heeded Him.
My memories of life, cut deep like a knife,
    in the company of such sin.

I did not deserve, the Lord to serve,
    for all the wrongs I'd done.
The blood He had shed, clouded my head;
    sacrificing His innocent Son.

"Will you not bow, before me now,
and swear allegiance to me?
Come let us begin, sign your name herein,
and forever you shall be free."

As on I looked, there appeared a book,
thick and deep with names.
All written in blood, that I could judge,
all the souls that he had claimed.

It was quite my intent, his task circumvent,
and flee far, far from that place.
He so stared at me, that my soul did freeze—
a strange look upon his face.

But how should I write, for there was no sight,
of pen or pencil or quill.
So I stared at him, while the evil din,
of the demon band played still.

"You need no quill, this task to fulfill,
come shown to me your hand.
Once simple prick, with a sharpened stick,
and sign, is all I command.

"But do not delay, time fades away,
and soon the opportunity will pass.
Come sign it quick, with your blood so thick,
begin your power to amass.

"But first bow down, upon the ground,
    and give to me your vow.
As your Master I, will not deny,
    you anything here and now."

XXXVIII

When the frost glistens, I recall the prison,
    of the Devilish Mountain of Gold.
On bended knees, I pray God please,
    forever protect my soul.
For I know so well, that the Devil's bell,
    rings out when the Devil rides.
And all good men, whether foe or friend,
    take refuge and from him hide.

Fast flew my thoughts, lest I suffered loss,
    I must not bend my knee.
The demon band and its dissonance,
    fell silent at his decree.

In tense anticipation, our strained conversation,
    fell silent as we sat.
He looked at me and I at he,
    as the book to me he passed.

But I knew my role, to save my soul,
    I knew to outwit him.
So I searched my mind, that I might find,
    to beat that Devil of sin.

Then to my relief, like a falling leaf,
    I heard the softest voice.
My Lady of Green, had returned it seemed;
    my heart and soul rejoiced.

She guided me; she would set me free,
    I knew it in my heart.
Quiet in my ear, I bare could hear,
    the words she did impart.

I stood to say, as I surveyed,
    the lay of the Mountain cave.
The demon band, as I did stand,
    thought it would me all enslave.

But my Butterfly Green, my emerald Queen,
    had told me what to do.
So I asked him there, defying his stare,
    if what he said was true.

"Why do you doubt? In this redoubt,
    I am the Master of my time.
Ask what you will, I am Master still.
    What task would you me assign?"

I told him straight, that my father late,
    was all I could desire.
Return his soul and all this gold,
    could melt in his Hell's fire.

That was all I asked—but a simple task,
    well within his gift.
One single, man's soul and all his gold,
    I would quit and all dismiss.

"Oh no! Oh no! He stays below!
    He is mine—of that no doubt!
Neither you nor he, can set him free.
    He stays here or hereabout."

I asked once more but he ignored
    me and my request.
"Ask that not, yet ask me aught.
    That you must accept.

"All souls here, in this my sphere,
    are bound by my own rules.
That's how it is, 'though you might wish . . .
    Come take instead some jewels."

There then appeared, as the demons cheered,
    a mass of precious stones.
Diamonds and pearls, from the heart of the world,
    as the demons drooled and foamed.

"I know it all. From Adam's great fall,
    to the desires of every man.
Everyone's goal is to acquire gold,
    so do now whatever you can.

"You cannot resist so do not desist,
    from taking all your fill.
Let's feast together and live forever.
    I'll have your answer still.

"What minor task, what would you ask,
    that I know not the answer?
Come, now mention, whatever question,
    let us continue our banter.

"If I know not, of any or aught,
    or any question that you ask,
I shall return, from where he burns,
    your father from the dark."

So I asked of him, that man of sin,
    what could be more worthy,
than the stones around, lying on the ground,
    and return my homeward journey?

What hidden gem, in all that realm,
    that never a man had seen,
could fill men's hearts, like a gracious art,
    and fit to grant a Queen.

What precious gem, could help not harm,
    that never any man had seen?
What would men desire? What did they require?
    I thought of my Lady of Green.

"What folly this?" I heard him hiss,
    as he cast me a hateful glance.
"No gem has been that I have not seen."
    Around his demons pranced.

"What I hold dear, is not men's fear,
    no stones but pure men's souls."
He laughed aloud, to that demon crowd,
    "That's more precious than gold!"

Some grains of wheat, on which I did feast,
    living on my father's farm,
in my hand rolled, like nuggets of gold,
    a weapon that could him harm.

So I showed to he, that grain of wheat,
    and rubbed the husk from the seed.
There lay that grain, pure and plain,
    paining him and his breed.

XXXIX

The Devil, it's said is no beast of dread,
    but comes in cunning disguise.
His victims find that his manner is kind,
    belying the vision of their eyes.
And his tooth of gold, calls to their souls;
    they succumb to avarice.
Like a Jezebel, I've heard it tell,
    they pay the ultimate price.

"Worship me! And I'll set him free!
   That is my only price!"
Then he softened his voice, his guile deployed,
   disguising his avarice.

"His soul is mine as shall be thine,
   of that there is no doubt.
If you persist, your demand insist,
   your soul I shall rip out!"

But I stood firm, defying him.
   I showed to him once more,
the grain of wheat, on which men feast—
   by which they lay great store.

He was outwitted, his mouth twisted,
   as he accepted his defeat.
His hand he waved, my father saved,
   he appeared before my feet.

I raised him up, gave him a cup,
   of the Devil's blood-red wine.
Slowly he stirred, as my Lady's words,
   told me of her design.

My father restored, this was my reward,
   for taking her advice.
She always spoke true, the Devil to subdue—
   the victim of his own avarice.

Behind me appeared, a horse reared,
a stallion of deepest black.
On his back I placed, my father embraced,
the horse's flank I smacked.

Off they ran, far from that land—
the Mountain opened wide.
As quick as he appeared, he fast disappeared,
as I remained the mountain inside.

"What now?" he asked, "What good to ask,
for any other soul?
You have but one, your task is done,
now sign as you were told!"

I maintained my ruse, so I refused,
to obey his Hellish command.
I remained calm, exuding charm,
holding steadfastly to my plan.

The Devil sneered, his demons cheered,
he looked me in the eye.
"You'll stay forever, leave me never,
for you shall never die.

"The past is past, don't let it cast,
some shadow of cleverness,
in your mind, for I think you'll find,
you're a man, no more no less.

"You cannot conceive nor me deceive,
 so sign and let's be done.
Open the book and have a look,
 your name's the last one.

"You cannot win, so let us begin,
 to bring this tale to an end.
Sign your name, your master proclaim,
 and forever be my friend.

"Do not tempt Fate, for my power is great,
 none can before me stand.
I reign supreme, in my regime,
 the whole of this earth and land.

"No-one can win, so just give in,
 to what I now require.
No use delay, hear all I say,
 if you would evade Hell's fire."

But resolute I, I walked him by,
 as he sat before his banquet.
I turned my back, before I asked,
 my question of that bandit.

No-one could win, against that man of sin—
 these were his very words.
As I turned around, standing on that ground,
 as appeared a multitude of birds.

XXXX

When I now reflect, I heartily accept,
    how foolish I have been.
In the Mountain of Gold, languish men's souls—
    they never again are seen.
I would rare return for fear I burn,
    upon the Mountain trail.
If I heard that bell, why who can tell,
    if you should hear my tale?

Then my Lady of Green, upon that scene,
appeared in a flash of light.
With defiant eyes, a host of butterflies,
lit the cave with glorious light.

"He is not one, you are undone!"
She cried with outstretched hands.
The Devil drew back, fearing an attack.
"His freedom *I* shall grant!"

A light of green, to me it seemed,
filled that Mountain cave.
The jewels and gold, turned bitter cold,
like the face of that Devil knave.

"To him you lied," my Lady cried,
"but no more, for we are two.
And together we, shall banish thee,
to Hell as I speak true!

"So get thee hence, 'ere I commence,
to kill your demon horde.
When I am done, you'll be but one,
at the mercy of my sword.

"So release him now and I'll allow,
your demon host and you,
to return to Hell with your demon bell.
You know that I speak true."

But the Devil then, returned again,
　　to the belly of his friends.
And unprepared, he stood and stared,
　　contemplating his end.

But soon restored, he to that horde,
　　a wicked smile he shot.
But still he knew, not one but two,
　　had foiled his evil plot.

But my Lady knew, 'though she spoke true,
　　he yet could not be stilled.
'Though that demon crowd, hissed aloud,
　　she could not so easily kill.

The Devil himself, with his evil wealth,
　　only the Lord could destroy.
With all her might, in that glowing, green light,
　　all her strength she deployed.

"Quick, run and flee," she shouted to me,
　　"He cannot cause you harm.
I'll hold him here, so do not fear,
　　I still have power in my arms."

Another horse appeared, a mighty steer,
　　pure white and standing proud.
The butterflies and birds, heard all her words,
　　I released a scream out loud.

To the saddle I mounted, the ground we pounded,
    as I saw the Mountain open wide.
"Now come with me!" I cried to she,
    "Be gone! I must remain inside!

"To the river ride fast and when it's passed,
    you shall be safe again.
I would you rather, live with your father,
    than die with these vile men.

"I shall hold them here, 'til you are clear.
    So go! Do not look back.
On the Mountain trail, you cannot fail,
    with your father on his horse of black.

"Be gone! Be gone! Ride for the sun.
    Take care to cross the river.
Ride with speed, my counsel heed,
    and return here never!"

So I sped away, that dreadful day;
    my horse galloped fast and sure.
My father and I, did by and by,
    reach the valley verdure.

But when I looked back, at the Mountain black,
    and saw my Lady of Green,
she held them there, in that Mountain lair,
    as the cave closed on that scene.

And in her eye, I thought I spied,
    a tear of purest green.
I turned around, on the Devil's ground,
    but the cave was lost it seems.

XXXXI

I never did find, that cave confined,
    yet still I hear her cries.
As she held him there in the Devil's lair,
    true tears filled my eyes.
'Though I knew right then, that of all men,
    my father and I alone
had lived to tell, of the Devil's bell,
    and I knew my lady was gone.

Along the way, as the Devil did say,
    he was ever in my head.
He tormented me, with wicked glee,
    I wished I soon be dead.

But my father urged, with kindly words—
    they kept me sane and whole.
Ever we rode, towards our abode,
    steadfast to our home goal.

We rode through day, we never did stay,
    we rode through darkest night.
'Till the river we crossed, no moment we lost,
    we rode with all our might.

As the sun was rising, upon the horizon,
    I saw my dear, dear home.
My mother's mind, was restored in time,
    in the days I spent alone.

A kind of happiness, no more no less,
    fell upon us from that day.
If I sometimes thought, or adventure sought,
    I put them far away.

Yet still I wonder, of what lies yonder,
    perhaps another trail?
But soon I find some chore to bind
    me to some other tale.

We have no needs, for fortune indeed,
    has shone on us so long.
Our saddle-bags both, by my troth,
    were filled with the color of dawn.

For the Devils gold, those coins so cold,
    lay in our leather sacs.
And jewels and stones, we brought them home,
    in both our saddle-packs.

How they were there, I do not care,
    but not by my or father's hand.
And now I'm free, all I long to see,
    is the Mountain of the damned.

But jewels and gold—they have no soul,
    'though delightful to the eye.
Yet never I'll find, my Lady's kind,
    no matter how I try.

'Though riches abound, the saddest sound,
    is the tale my father tells.
Of the Mountain of Gold, dead men's soul,
    and the Devil's Golden Bell.

EPILOGUE

Sometimes it seems, a flash of Green,
flits by my peripheral vision.
Then my heart beats slow, my soul's laid low,
for her voice I intently listen.

Like a Summer sky, when the clouds are high,
the air is silent and still.
It's then I hear her voice so dear,
calming my troubled will.

She gave up all in that Mountain tall,
that I might live to tell,
of my quest for gold, tortured souls,
and the ringing of that bell.

And so good Sir, now that you've heard,
my wonderous tale of gold,
will you hear one more, as of before?
How would you have it told?

From your doubting eyes and disapproving sighs,
it seems you do not believe
that the Devil was tested, tried and bested.
Such a tale you cannot conceive.

Well, it is the truth, that this wretched youth,
    has related to you this day.
But now I am older, wiser and bolder,
    so I'll depart and be on my way.

But do not despair, we shall all meet there,
    each on our Mountain trail.
For if Fortune and you, drink the Devil's brew,
    perhaps you'll tell me your tale?

But who is your friend? Whose coin you spend,
    in this stinking saloon of old?
I see when he smiles, tribulations and trials,
    and . . . a solitary tooth of gold.

www.ingramcontent.com/pod-product-compliance
Lightning Source LLC
Chambersburg PA
CBHW070616310726
48982CB00001B/100

* 9 7 8 1 7 2 5 2 8 0 6 8 7 *